T0194007

KNOWING
GOD MORE

KNOWING
GOD MORE

AN INTROSPECTIVE 40 DAY GUIDE

DAN HOLLOWAY

 iUniverse®

KNOWING GOD MORE
AN INTROSPECTIVE 40 DAY GUIDE

New Revised Standard Version Bible, copyright © 1989 the Division of Christian Education of the National Council of the Churches of Christ in the United States of America. Used by permission. All rights reserved.

The Holy Bible, English Standard Version. ESV® Text Edition: 2016. Copyright © 2001 by Crossway Bibles, a publishing ministry of Good News Publishers.

Scripture taken from the New King James Version®. Copyright © 1982 by Thomas Nelson. Used by permission. All rights reserved.

iUniverse books may be ordered through booksellers or by contacting:

iUniverse
1663 Liberty Drive
Bloomington, IN 47403
www.iuniverse.com
1-800-Authors (1-800-288-4677)

ISBN: 978-1-5320-9892-5 (sc)
ISBN: 978-1-5320-9893-2 (e)

Print information available on the last page.

iUniverse rev. date: 04/09/2020

CONTENTS

ACKNOWLEDGMENTS

Ideas shared in this book came from over twenty-five years of presenting Sunday lessons (we don't call them sermons) at church. More specifically, they come from living life in discovery mode. In order to produce a lesson, I always needed to find a spark – something that made the subject interesting to me. I could not imagine sitting through a boring sermon like I had to when growing up. I needed to find what I called "the juice." What new perspective could I find that was exciting to me, and then hopefully exciting to my congregation? I became quite the metaphysical observer. I looked for meaning in circumstances large and small, in people's reactions and responses to all that life dealt them.

I am grateful to Spirit for opening my eyes, at least somewhat, to what life was offering me. Every Sunday was like a chance to share a new secret to living more fully. It might have been about the power of forgiveness, or an opportunity to prove spiritual principles through combining one's faith with limitless imagination. So I say Thank You God, for the "Juice" in my life!

I am also blessed with a loving and patient wife, who provided space for me to do my work and encouragement to move forward, even when I had doubts about my own ability. Thank you, Kathy McManus! (Actually, Rev. Kathy McManus! – She is also an ordained Unity minister.) I probably would not have gotten this book to print without the support of my life coach, Rev. Sharon

Connors, who motivated me, and who called me on my "stuff" and would not let me slide through life. I am also so grateful for my editor, Diane Bressner, for helping to bring order to the chaos of my writing and offering valuable and supportive ideas. Appreciation is also due to Brenda Moreu, my church office manager, whose positive attitude and dedication was a constant mainstay.

Thanks to all who showed me the importance of living a life with purpose and meaning. I am grateful – and I am still learning!

Thank you all!
Rev. Dan Holloway

In the Bible, the number 40 has special significance. Generally speaking, 40 represents the amount of time it takes to accomplish something. Noah's ark was in the flooded waters for 40 days. Moses led the Israelites through the wilderness for 40 years. Jesus went off by himself for 40 days at the beginning of his ministry.

How long it takes you to read this book and apply the *Steps for Deeper Understanding* is, of course, up to you. I have simply broken this time down to 40 days in order to allow for time to consider the topic and the questions, as well as to open a process of spiritual evolution. I bless you on your way to know God more!

Let us begin with an exploration of the will of God.

Many times I simply do not understand the big picture. I cannot figure out why certain things happen and other things don't. For instance, people have asked since the beginning of time why suffering exists, or why life is often so confusing. We would like all of life to make sense so we would know what to do, and how and when to do it.

But life does not work that way. Life happens. We each have our up times and our down times — and occasionally even those times are confusing. I have had many people tell me, "You know, at the time, I thought that (whatever: the job loss, illness, divorce) was terrible, but now I see it was a real blessing, perhaps in disguise."

All this confusion has made me wonder what God's will *is*, after all. I shared my best answer in a Sunday lesson with my congregants. I told them that I had come across a very old document that explained the will of God. (I may have embellished here.) I submit the following for your consideration.

THE LAST WILL AND TESTAMENT OF GOD

Please do not mistakenly think that because my will is being read I am gone. I am always here and available. This is not only the last will and testament but also the first will and testament of God. My will is always the same. It does not change. My will is the creative force. I will, and it is so. This same creative force is in you. What you will, manifests. How and what you apply the power of will to is demonstrated in your world, both the inner and the outer world, the world of cause and of effect, the world of thought and the world of deed.

My will is to be expressed. You can carry out my will. I can and do express in you, and through you, and even as you. You are made in my image and likeness. Just as a child expresses its parents' traits, so you express mine.

As love, you express through acts of kindness, acceptance of others, forgiveness, and harmony. As strength, you express through courage, commitment, and willingness to grow. As faith, you express as an underlying belief in good, in possibilities for greater things for yourself and for others, and as spiritual understanding which surpasses human intellect.

A testament is a testimony, a proof of sorts. You have heard my will. My will is to be expressed. The testament is where you come in.

You are to be and demonstrate the proof of God. You have all that you need to do that: the Christ within. You are the testament. Prove me in your life. Prove me as your life. Let me make your world better through you, one moment, one divine idea, at a time.

My will is your will.

My testament is _you._

Signed in the eternal moment,
God

AWARENESS

All of our possibilities for positive change must begin with awareness. We cannot address what we do not see. We cannot change what we do not acknowledge. Yet so much of our time is spent on autopilot. We have developed routines — how we travel to work or to a friend's place, how we begin our day, or even how we react or respond to outer circumstances — and in our robotic ways we give up true awareness. We may notice the light, but not appreciate the sunrise. We may notice the temperature but not really breathe in all the subtleties of the air. So we begin our journey with the simple task of becoming aware first of our surroundings, and then of our thoughts, feelings, and actions.

IDENTITY

Continue to be who and how you are, to astonish a mean world with your acts of kindness. Continue to allow humor to lighten the burden of your tender heart.

— *Maya Angelou*

Just who, exactly, do you think you are? More importantly, why do you think that? Identity is often more a matter of personality rather than individuality. In other words, who we think we are seems to change with the conditions around us. We may measure success by comparing what we have and where we are in life versus others' life conditions. And we may look for the faults or weaknesses in others so we may feel better about ourselves. In truth, of course, who we are has nothing to do with anyone else. Our personality can change, but who we really are, our individuality, the spirit of us, does not change. We simply grow into our awareness of it. Hopefully.

DAY 1: DO-BE-DO-BE-DO

What do you want to be when you grow up? I remember hearing that asked of me when I was a child. Sometimes, quite frankly, I still wonder. My dad showed me his high school yearbook long ago where the students had written of their aspirations. Some planned to be doctors, or lawyers, or business leaders. Dad wanted to be a cowboy. And he was, for a few years anyway. He participated in rodeos, roping steers, and so forth, kind of a "Hop-along Holloway" sort.

Well, Dad continued to grow up. He went into the paint business, traveling all over the country, selling to distributors. Dad also had scientific interests and invented a few things in his industry. For example, he devised putting primary colors and black and white onto fan blades and adjusting the dials to ascertain exactly how much of which colors were needed to match the color of the spinning fan. Dad was in the sales business, but that is not what he *was*. That was what he *did*.

We get that distinction mixed up quite a bit. We think we are what we do. How would you describe yourself, if asked? Would you begin with your gender, age, and occupation, or maybe your interests, physical location, and education? All of these details may help describe us, but they are more about what we do than who we are.

We label ourselves and others in so many ways. These labels automatically do two things: they limit us, and they cause us to compare ourselves to others.

In the third chapter of Exodus, Moses asks God's name. God answers, "I AM WHO I AM." (I'm not shouting —that's how it's written in the Bible.) "Thus you shall say to the Israelites, 'I AM has sent me to you.'" When we say "I am" we are, in essence, using the name of God. Further, the Hebrew word shared as 'I am' is *hayah* [pronounced "haw-yaw"]. This word means "I am," but can also mean "I am becoming." I would like to think I am always in a place of becoming, that there is more to know, to learn, and to express in order for me to fulfill my purpose in this life.

The subconscious mind believes what it is told. Whenever we say "I am" followed by words like stupid, foolish, sick, or even sad, tired, angry, or sorry, we are defining ourselves. But we are not stupid, and we are not sad, tired, or any of those other adjectives. That is not what or whom we *are*, but rather what we are *experiencing*. We may feel apologetic, but that feeling does not make us a sorry person: that is to say, it is not the whole of who we are.

The "I am" of us is always seeking expression through us. The activity of Spirit, of God, wants to be made manifest through us. We are the conduit through which God does some of God's work. Rather than declaring we are sad, angry, or sorry persons, we can acknowledge that we *feel* sad, angry, or sorry, a subtle but profound discernment.

In truth, we are each and all spiritual beings. A spark of divinity lies within each of us. God expresses not only all around us, but also through us, to others. For instance, many people say that God is love. As we demonstrate unconditional love to others, through kindness, compassion, understanding, and patience, we are expressing God-love.

While I am not telling you something you do not already know, I would guess that many of you regularly misuse those two simple words, "I am." As you do, you are putting energy on whatever follows those words. "I am a healthy, loving, and worthy person" is an affirmation that uplifts, while "I am worthless" or "I am never going to get this right" creates a drag on the spirit.

Remember: *You are a divine spiritual creation expressing through your humanity.* Align with the Divine. The more we use our words and thoughts to express the higher truth of us, we demonstrate two pivotal ideas: We are more than "human doings," and we are always in the process of becoming.

5

Steps for Deeper Understanding

If someone were to describe you, what words would they use? Do you think they would describe what you do and did, or who you really are?

How are you using your "I am?" Notice which times you are saying "I am" when you could be expressing the same thought using the words "I feel."

Breathe in deeply and feel your connection with the Divine. It is within you!

Notes:_____

_____

_____

_____

DAY 2: YOU ARE UNIQUE, JUST LIKE EVERYONE ELSE

In nature, we celebrate diversity. Our planet contains an estimated 8.7 million different species: 10,000 kinds of birds, 400,000 kinds of flowers, and over 1.5 million species of animals on Earth, with 10,000 additional species being discovered each year!

Yet for all we appreciate in nature, we often look upon other people, and our diversity as human beings, and find fault.

All people are created with sacred worth. Many, if not most, people could agree with that statement.

However, many people judge others as unworthy because *they* (the others) don't believe in the same things, or in the same way. *They* didn't grow up with the correct religious or political values. *They* and *their kind* are a threat to all we hold dear.

We spend far too much time identifying and labeling what is not like us.

You are unique — just like everyone else. We have so much in common that looking for all the reasons we are different, is a waste of energy, especially if the purpose is to make someone wrong or to make us right.

Ancient skull studies generally agree that we all came from Africa 200,000 or more years ago. The first people grew in number and split into different tribes. Over time, clans and tribes fought each other for survival. As they looked for ways to identify their own, humans also became being pretty good at identifying those who weren't their own.

The differentiation of "the other" still continues today. Many cultures, religions, institutions, and systems of belief require a strict way of thinking and believing that aligns with *their* way. The consequences of failure, of doing or saying something against the code, are dire. One can be shunned, outcast, ostracized, and excommunicated. Families can be broken up, forced to choose between their blood relatives and their spiritual family, and (often,

7

they are warned) between acceptance in the next life and eternal damnation.

While I don't understand it completely, I acknowledge that my way of seeing the world is not going to be the same as another's. My way feels right to me, but that does not make another's way wrong. After all, we can learn so much from each other, from our differences, and from our oneness. *We all share the same experience of being human, even if we don't share the identical human experience*.

We are not born with prejudice. We grow into prejudice through the principles of teaching and learning. Therefore, if we choose, we can grow out of prejudice with new awareness. We can retrain our minds.

We are continually looking for ways to better our shared experience of each other.

Sometimes, in some ways, we may feel excluded. Comedian George Gobel famously said, "Some days I feel like the whole world is a tuxedo, and I'm a pair of brown shoes." At times we may feel very alone, certain that no one else could really understand what we're going through. In truth, everyone has had feelings of loneliness; everyone has had heartache. Nearly everyone has had health, prosperity, or self-esteem challenges from time to time.

But we can get through these times with faith, with patience, with acceptance, and with each other. Acceptance allows us to make a safe place for others to share their feelings about their challenges without making it a contest. Acceptance allows us to celebrate our diversity as well as our oneness. We can simply choose to demonstrate a little kindness. We keep our hand off the car horn and exhibit a bit more patience. Being more forgiving, accepting, loving, and helpful can be easy. Simply remember:

You are not alone. You are unique, just like everyone else.

Steps for Deeper Understanding

List, in your mind, at least three ways you are a unique human being.

List, in your mind, at least three ways those whose values and ways vastly differ from yours are unique human beings.

List in your mind or on paper as many ways as you can think of that people are alike.

Notes:_____

_____

_____

_____

DAY 3: BLOOM WHERE YOU
ARE PLANTED

I once heard of a man who read that he was much more likely to be involved in a car accident within five miles of his home — so he moved!

Of course, that's a joke, but it's no joke that we think making outer changes in life will solve all our problems. Change needs to be an inside job before outer change can be lasting. We sometimes think that by simply changing outer circumstances we will change our life. So we look for something new, the next best thing, place, or person — blouse, house, or spouse.

Among other activities, we are here to grow our souls, which means we must grow our consciousness. But we can't do that growing if we continually seek to escape the opportunities/challenges that life is offering us. We may sometimes feel beleaguered by difficulties. However, if we choose to adjust our perspective, we may see that the universe is bringing to us exactly what we need at the time. Remember that wherever we are, God is, too.

Many years ago, I quit a well-paying job that I hated. I started my own business, which failed shortly thereafter. I took on various sales positions over the next year, but nothing really fit. I was trying to make changes in my life by making outer changes, but I was unwilling or unable to make any inner changes. Shortly before the end of the year I felt miserable and at my wits' end. I remember making telephone sales calls, praying that no one would really pick up the phone on the other end of the line because I really did not want to talk to them. I needed to find a different line of work, something that would allow my creative juices to flow.

I prayed for the right and perfect job to appear, letting God know I was ready, I was available, and I had faith God would point the way! My prayers were answered in the most unexpected way. I got a call from a friend who told me about a part-time, temporary job that was not a pure sales commission-type job. I went through the "intense" (about two hours) training and resigned myself to work this minimum wage job that I seriously wondered what I had done to deserve.

But something happened — a miracle of sorts, really. *I remembered that this job was the answer to prayer* and simply surrendered to the process. I was inspired to treat this job as if it were the best-paying job in the world. Suddenly, my energy shifted. I stood taller, I was friendly with everyone around me, and I did my work with pride and dignity. I got my first promotion in three days, off the phones and assisting the manager. A few months later I had the opportunity to apply at the same company for a permanent full-time job. Within six months, I had earned six promotions, becoming a project manager over six supervisors with a total of 200 employees.

I learned to "Let Go and Let God" be in charge. I got myself and my ego out of the way, choosing instead to bloom where I was planted. Once I surrendered, the universe conspired to support me in ways I could not have imagined. I didn't need to change everything around me. *I only needed to change myself,* and all things started working together for good.

Steps for Deeper Understanding

In your current life circumstances where do you generally find your frustrations?

How would your life be different if you discovered your frustrations to really be somehow in your favor?

Decide on one thing, at least for today, you can choose to see differently.

Notes:_____

_____

_____

_____

PERSPECTIVE

Change the story and you change perception; change perception and you change the world.

—*Jean Houston*

Things are never absolutely as they seem. There is always more to any condition or event than what we see. In light of this fact, it makes sense to at least have a willingness to see things from other perspectives. Doing so makes us wiser, more compassionate, and more able to make healthy, just decisions.

DAY 4: ALL THINGS WORK TOGETHER FOR GOOD

I often sign off my emails with a quote from Romans 8:28 that states "all things work together for good, for those who love God, who are called according to his purpose."

I find this quote particularly reassuring when things do not seem to be working well. For instance, the other day I found out that my air duct from the clothes dryer was filled with 11 years' worth of lint and that is why clothes were not drying properly. The next day the water heater stopped heating water. Two days later I found out that I had a broken pipe leading from the house to the city sewer system. Today, my exercise watch battery died: the watch face just turned black. Now, tell me, how are all things working together for good?

Robert Fulghum, author of *All I Really Need to Know I Learned in Kindergarten,* also wrote "Sigmund Wollman's Reality Test." In that piece, the author shared that he (Fulghum) had worked at a resort as a young man. One evening, he became very upset. Every day, all the employees were fed the same thing: wieners and sauerkraut with stale rolls. Finally, he couldn't take it anymore. He let off steam for 20 minutes. He could not believe anyone could treat employees so badly! Hearing him, Sigmund Wollman commented wisely, "If you break your neck, if you have nothing to eat, if your house is on fire, then you've got a problem. Everything else is inconvenience. Life *is* inconvenient. Learn to separate the inconveniences from real problems."

I believe so much of our life experience has to do with our attitude. Our energy attracts energy, whether positive or negative. Why stay in misery if you can back off from it, even a little? You may actually see light at the end of the tunnel, and it's <u>not</u> a train heading your way! For me and my piddly difficulties, I chose to take care of the business I needed to take care of, but not to get overly upset or concerned about it.

I found out that through Amazon.com I could buy a cleaner for the dryer lint that would extend to 20 feet. The water heater, never a problem before, only required hitting a reset button, at least for now. The plumbing? That would take replacing some pipes at some cost. Luckily, however, I have a plumber friend who will do this at a fair price. Also, a watch battery costs only a couple of dollars.

So much for household repairs. What about the things that happen in life that seem to be tumultuous?

I have faced health issues in the past, and certainly have ministered to many, many people who faced serious health challenges. I have spoken to people who could find no reason to continue living. I have spent countless hours counseling people who were facing relationship problems. Should I have told each of them that all things were working together for good?

Generally, no. People in the midst of their difficulties are not receptive to such talk. But I can know this truth for them, and I can hold a centered and peaceful prayer for them while they deal with their emotions, their fears, their blame, their regrets, and their shame.

The Truth (with a capital "T") is bigger than all of their despair. Healing does happen. I have often heard people sharing about past challenges. They say that at the time, they were feeling helpless, hopeless even. They did not know what to do. And they wondered why this, whatever *this* was, had to happen.

Looking back, though, they often saw that without facing and moving through their problems, they would not have gained the strength, the understanding, or the patience that they gained. They would not have met the people they met or discovered new ways to make life happen for them. They have gained wisdom that comes from living life and seeing their way through not only the tough times, but also the good times.

Yes, we will have difficulties in life, but we don't want or need to make them bigger than they really are. Mark Twain once said, "I am an old man and have known a great many troubles, but most of them have never happened."

Whether you are facing problems in life — and many of you are — or you are plagued with inconveniences, please know, or at least be open to the possibility, that all things work together for good.

Steps for Deeper Understanding

What have you faced in the past that felt daunting at the time? What have you learned from that time in your life?

What have you been considering a difficulty or challenge, when in reality it is merely an inconvenience?

Today, consider an area of your life where you can demonstrate peace where there is unrest, or where you can find joy or acceptance, realizing in all things you have the power of choice.

Notes:_____

_____

_____

_____

DAY 5: DON'T GIVE UP — SURRENDER!

"Uncle! I give up!" my seven-year-old self cried out as my ten-year-old brother pinned me to the ground. "Uncle!" He was in the habit of demonstrating his older-brother-ness, and I unwillingly complied. I wish I could say my experience in giving up ended there, but it taught me, unfortunately, that it's often easier to give up than to struggle or fight. It didn't occur to me until much later that there is an alternative.

We probably all feel the desire to "give up" sometimes, when it looks like our task or challenge is overbearing or our goal is improbable to attain. We may go from being frustrated to downright disheartened. We may have decided that the effort just isn't worthwhile. But what happens when we simply give up? We miss out on so many potential possibilities for good to happen in our lives.

We are not given ideas and opportunities without also being given the help we need to make them manifest into reality. An inspired idea comes to us filled with spiritual potential that, combined with faith, imagination, and commitment, yields positive results. Even a seeming setback can be an expression of divine timing.

So, what else can we do when faced with our obstacles, challenges, and seeming limitations? Rather than giving up, perhaps we want to consider surrendering. There is a difference. I am not speaking of the hands-in-the-air, waving-the-white-flag kind of surrendering, but rather surrendering our insistence or resistance.

Too often, great possibilities are quashed before they even begin to be expressed because we need to have things "our way." I have heard it said that we can either be standing in the way of God, or we can *be* the way of God. We can be nonresistant to the flow of circumstances, flexible in the face of seeming challenges, and faith-filled in the potential for a positive outcome. Our willingness and our efforts combine to open the way for Spirit to express in our lives. We are not victims of life but participants, and we can prove that surrendering to new, higher, greater ideas eliminates perceived limitations.

For instance, a woman recently told me she wanted more financial freedom, but she was on a fixed income. Who fixed it? Who limits the universe of positive possibilities to show up in such small ways? Only we do, with our words, our actions, and our beliefs. In truth, our possibilities are as great as the imagination, faith, and commitment we apply to our life circumstances.

Certainly, we have difficulties in life, and we can prove to anyone why we need to either struggle or to give up; but we can also prove to ourselves and anyone interested that surrendering is a wise choice. We are not surrendering to the circumstances, nor to another person, but to the Higher Power we must believe wants only our best. This kind of surrender brings inner peace, opens us to a fresh outlook, and provides an instant removal of the emotion of desperation. Let us notice the words we use to describe our challenges and opportunities. These words have power. They have life. As we decide to live life more fully, without constant struggle, we surrender into our highest good.

Steps for Deeper Understanding

Identify an area of your life that feels overwhelming, where you have considered giving up.

Become clear on the seeming obstacles. Define them. Give them words.

Notice where you have insistence or resistance. Is there some part of you that is able to simply surrender to a new understanding? Let it unfold naturally and feel the freedom of surrender.

Notes:_____

_____

_____

_____

DAY 6: FREE TO BE YOU AND ME

Independence Day has special meaning for many of us. We value our freedom, individually and collectively. Freedom is an important part of our country's identity. We each have freedom to be who we really are, to express ourselves as we are guided, and to live life as fully as we can.

I seek to live by this mission statement: To demonstrate peace, joy, acceptance, and the power of choice. Of course, I cannot express any of these genuinely unless I truly feel them myself. Yet when life feels a bit crazy or chaotic, peace may seem distant.

In the midst of turmoil, I take a breath and concentrate quickly on two actions: put the situation in perspective and take charge of my power of imagination. As immediate and difficult as some incidents may seem, I can always focus on the bigger picture. I can choose to see details from a different point of view, or at least have faith that all will work out somehow, even if I am clueless as to how or when that will happen. I can remember past circumstances that were daunting at the time. Yet I miraculously came through them. I have found that situations are generally not as bad as they may first appear. This gives me hope and confidence to do whatever I am called to do. For instance, I once fell while playing tennis, going for the perfect return. I dislocated my arm. My first thought was "This is not good. My arm should definitely be closer to my shoulder!" My second thought was "Did I make the shot? Rats! I didn't." I did, however, have a proficient person at a clinic place my arm back where it needed to be, without the stress or pain I feared I might have had to endure.

What about joy? How do you find joy when you are dealing with anger or sadness or fear? The answer is that you don't. All emotions are to be felt. What keeps us from joy? We tend to stay in the other emotions, needlessly magnifying them by reliving an incident in our mind or justifying our feelings to others to gain support for our misery. We can each find things in life to kindle any emotion. Why stay in a place that feels bad any longer than you need to? Feel the feelings, certainly, but then move on. You have a life to live!

Acceptance is the third part of my mission. Acceptance does not mean suffering silently through life circumstances, nor does it mean taking no action when conditions call for action. Acceptance simply means (1) I accept people for who they are and where they are without feeling the need to change them into someone more acceptable to me (unless they are seeking change, of course); (2) I accept the conditions of my life, at least as a starting point. *That's what's so — so what?* Only by accepting and not resisting or ignoring my circumstances can I take steps to change them for the better; and (3) I accept myself as I am, with all my seeming faults and flaws, knowing that I am not here to compare myself to others, but to do the best I can with what I have been given.

Lastly, I realize the greatest gift: the power of choice. I am free to make good choices as well as those that do not turn out so well. I learn (hopefully, at least eventually) from my choices. Free will allows each of us to choose how we will live life. Yes, differing physical traits, natural abilities, and levels of income exist, but everyone has a choice of attitude. We can see the glass half empty, half full, or completely full of two things (water and air, for example). My mission is to demonstrate peace, joy, acceptance, and the power of choice. I choose peace. I choose joy. I choose acceptance. Please, if you are so guided, join me.

Steps for Deeper Understanding

What's seems to be holding you down or holding you back at this point in your life?

How would it look to simply accept what is, at least in this moment, without feeling the absolute need to change it?

When you come from a place of nonresistance rather than insisting on your own way, new ideas or perspectives appear. Open to them today.

Notes:_____

_____

_____

_____

DAY 7: WE ARE MAGNETS AND MIRRORS

I probably have ten mirrors around the house. Like most people, I want to make sure my hair is in place, my teeth have no spinach particles, and my tie is straight. How we look is important to most of us. But how we look is not the same as how we see.

How do we look at life's circumstances, and what do we see? Author Ken Keyes wrote in *Handbook of Higher Consciousness*, "A loving person lives in a loving world. A hostile person lives in a hostile world. Everyone you meet is your mirror." When you approach others with a sense of joy or serenity, that will likely be reflected back to you. When you come at others with anger, frustration, or fear, then that is likely what you will see.

How do you see your world? Do you start the day with "Good Morning, God" or "Good God, it's morning!"? A country song wryly asserts, "If it weren't for bad luck, I'd have no luck at all." Luckily, we have been blessed with free will. We can choose how we will see our days, our relationships, our lives. I choose to believe that holding a positive attitude can never hurt. Not all things are good, of course, but good can be found in even the most difficult circumstances. In disasters, for instance, people come together to provide help and comfort. In everyday happenings, we choose our attitude, which helps create all the difference.

Certainly, we can gripe and grumble. We can find much to complain about and plenty of people to share our upset and our grievances with. Interestingly, however, we can also find much to appreciate. We simply must look for it. We find what we look for.

We can learn about ourselves by noticing what we notice, by stepping back and observing where we put our attention. If we don't like what we see, we simply look elsewhere. The mirrors are all around us.

We are not only mirrors, but we are also magnets. We draw to us much of what is happening in life through our thoughts and feelings. Are we feeling and thinking about abundance or about lack, about appreciation or about envy? A Unity belief affirms that "thoughts held in mind produce after their kind." The beauty in this universal spiritual truth is that we can take charge of our lives at any time. We simply focus on what we want to draw to us. We become "spiritual magnets" through our thoughts and feelings. Equally beautiful is that we can prove this in our own lives.

Notice what you notice. Notice how you respond or react to the happenings in your day. When you experience an inconsiderate driver, are you filled with righteous indignation, or do you send them a prayerful thought? Too often we carry the burden of our upset with an incident much longer than we need to. The happiest, healthiest people are not that way because of outer conditions, but because of the choices they make when dealing with outer conditions. They look for and find a more positive way.

We find what we look for. How simple is that? Let's look for what we want to have in life and appreciate all that is working well.

Steps for Deeper Understanding

Today, notice without judgment how people are responding or reacting to you.

In what ways do your life circumstances and the people you encounter reflect your attitudes and ways of being?

Celebrate the positive, and where you feel challenged, consider the benefits of making some changes — not for others, necessarily, but for the greater good.

Notes:_____

_____

_____

_____

LIVING IN THE MOMENT

The power for creating a better future is contained in the present moment: You create a good future by creating a good present.

— *Eckhart Tolle*

I often find myself distracted by so many things — email, traffic, TV, upsets about something that happened, concerns about something that may happen. All these distractions keep me from living in the present moment, *if I let them!* Luckily, I have a choice. With a bit of work and a decision to live consciously, I can be in this moment, right now. I can appreciate the power that comes from being fully present. That's where I want to live. And so I will.

DAY 8: ON LIVING IN THE MOMENT

Have you noticed that things don't always turn out the way you expect? You may have heard the saying "We make plans, and God laughs." We do our best, of course, and then life happens. The other day, my wife Kathy and I were kayaking, enjoying the beauty all around us when I looked down and saw a manatee swimming under my little boat. As slow as a manatee is, I am even slower maneuvering a kayak, but, luckily, we did not touch. While many in these parts of Florida have had manatee encounters, this was a first for us, and we could hardly contain our excitement. I whipped out my little Canon camera in its waterproof case to take shots of this incredible creature.

Another manatee, twice as large as the first, came swimming by, and I took more pictures, mainly movies. Finally a third manatee began playing: swimming up to us, poking his little nose out of the water, turning, twisting, doing back flips, and then retreating to the edge of the water near the sand to rest for a minute. We named him Marvin. Marvin entertained us for about half an hour. I took so many movies, certain some would turn out beautifully. But little did I know I had sabotaged myself just a few days before.

Although I had owned my camera for a few years, I had never really read the handbook. I would aim, zoom, and hit the button. It worked. Then, when I suddenly developed an interest in making better pictures, I actually studied the directions, learning all kinds of things that would have helped me had I known before. I was convinced that all my camera skills were working out much better this day, until I got home and looked at my results. I had switched the movie selection on "time lapse" photography, a feature that would, for example, shorten a minute-long movie to a few seconds. This setting was for filming flowers opening up in the morning sun or the slow nighttime crossing of the moon in the sky, not for taking pictures of gentle sea creatures.

I am convinced that *National Geographic* will not tap me on the shoulder for any photography help. I made one of the slowest creatures in the world move through the water like a speedboat.

In all this, however, I see a lesson. Really. I was, of course, disappointed in my results. Yet I also was able to figure out what I did wrong; and with the help of a few movie programs on my computer, I was able to extract some fascinating "still" photos from my time-lapse results. The lesson, though, was that the pictures were not as important as the experience. I can remember the moments and truly appreciate them. The pictures were just a small memento. They did not capture the smile on Kathy's face, the feel of the light breeze or the sunlight, the splashes of water, or the wonder of nature.

Being caught up in the busyness of life so much that we miss the beauty of the moment is easy if we allow it. We can get just as caught up in our expectations of life's circumstances. Remembering to live in conscious awareness and in appreciation of all of life, moment by moment, is living fully. Things don't always turn out the way we expect, but that's kind of what we expected, isn't it?

Steps for Deeper Understanding

What are you doing today that you might be doing "automatically"?

Can you consciously notice the thoughts and feelings you are currently experiencing?

Make a point to find the beauty in some aspect of your life today.

Notes:_____

_____

_____

_____

DAY 9: A FRESH START

Each of us would like to have a fresh start in some area of life: a rift in a relationship, a preventable health issue, a passed-up job opportunity or one we should not have accepted. Maybe we are being called to start something we never before attempted, but always wanted to do, such as learn a language, play a musical instrument, enroll in art classes, or take up tennis.

We cannot change the past, of course, but we can change the way we see the past. Instead of living in regret, we can see our past as a series of learning experiences. We have become better people because of our past, especially if we look for the positive. Yes, finding the positive in certain accomplishments, or in overcoming difficult obstacles, may be easy, but what if every action had the seed of positivity within it?

The passing of a loved one, for instance, can have the positive aspect of appreciation for the influence that person had on your life. You learned, you loved, you valued the relationship. The loved one is not forgotten. Any loss is a loss because of the value you assigned to it. But dwelling on the feelings that accompany loss is non-productive. We can feel those feelings and move through them in time. But they need not define us.

A therapist friend once talked to me about the loss of my father. She said that often we are dealing with two types of loss, and we really need to focus on just one. The one we need not hold onto is the *loss of what could have been*. We can never know that, and to be preoccupied by what could have been is a misuse of our imagination. Let us instead live through our challenge and move forward, stronger because of our experience. Yes, the move can be difficult, but move on we must. As Mother Teresa once famously confided, "I know God won't give me anything I can't handle. I just wish that he didn't trust me so much."

Sometimes fresh starts are of our own volition, but sometimes not. I would like to think that I am able to listen to that "still, small voice" of inner calling to begin again or begin anew. I would like to think that as I receive that calling, the path is already laid out before me. Following my guidance, and remaining open to synchronous and serendipitous events, all things are falling together for me. Author Napoleon Hill told us, "Whatever the mind can conceive and believe, it can achieve."

Faith allows us to open to all we can imagine. We imagine success in a fresh start, whether it is developing certain skills and talents, healing a relationship, or simply becoming clear on what to do to become all we came here to become. We combine our faith with our imagination to see and feel all the positive possibilities. But that is not enough.

Although "faith" and "trust" are often used interchangeably, these words can be interpreted in very different ways. Faith believes in the possibilities but makes no real move forward. Only when we trust, do we take the risk to live more fully, to "take the plunge," to make the call, to write the letter or the book, to take the class. A fresh start is what revitalizes us, gives us hope, and makes life worth living. It is my prayer this day, as you read this, you are filled with hope, positive anticipation, and faith, and that you will trust Spirit and yourself as you rededicate yourself to be all you are here to be!

Steps for Deeper Understanding

In what area of your life would you like to have a fresh start?

Listen to your guidance. What is one next step you can identify to begin anew?

Envision the best possible result and make an action plan to take that step.

Notes:_____

_____

_____

_____

DAY 10: INSTANT REPLAY

We really value our time, don't we? I recently flew 2500 miles from Florida to California. The whole flying time was about five hours. *Amazing.* We buy fast food. We eat instant oatmeal. We record television programs so we can rush through the commercials to save precious time and avoid being "sold." I am sure many people either mute or speed through campaign commercials. After you see one or two, they get old quickly.

Now we have Instant Replay. As fast as our lives go, we still feel the need to go back and replay certain scenes on a TV show if we missed a word or two or if we want to review a sports play.

But would you want Instant Replay for the times and circumstances of your life? "Did they really say that?" we might ask. "Let's play that back and watch again. Did I see what I thought I saw? Did he really run that light? Did she actually snub me?" *Inquiring minds want to know.*

While it might be handy to assess the actions of others, Instant Replay for life would mean that our own actions could be scrutinized. We might actually need to admit we made a mistake from time to time!

More than a bit of humility is necessary for anyone's decisions to be meticulously examined for mistakes.

Actually, we do have Instant Replay. We have it in our minds, and we use it all the time. Generally, though, we do not have all the cameras rolling. In sports, we can see action from many different angles, an ability that tremendously helps our capacity to assess a situation. In life, we often stick to one angle, one perspective.

If we are to really develop a greater understanding of situations, of others, and of ourselves, we must be willing to see from different perspectives, not just one view. We must be teachable and humble. We do not learn unless we are willing to make a few errors along the way. Living life too safely is not living.

One way to see our circumstances is from the viewpoint that somehow, any situation has at least one positive perspective. Every situation contains the seed of a blessing that must be nurtured to be fully realized. Willingness to make peace with our past is helpful. Too often we repeatedly replay the scene from a difficult time when we were hurt or insulted or angered. Of course, if we don't use a different angle or perspective, we get the same results.

Why play those painful times over and over again? We can't change yesterday, and we can't really predict tomorrow with certainty. I have two friends, husband and wife, are among the healthiest people I know. Within a week, they both ended up in the hospital for completely different reasons. One got a tick bite from a trip to Virginia and developed complications. The other slipped, fell, and ruptured her spleen. No one would have predicted either situation.

They are both doing well now, in part due to their resilience and their attitude. They are simply unwilling to replay their misery over and over. Once or twice should do, and then let's get on with life!

While we can't change events, we can remember that we are the ones who give meaning to whatever happens in our lives. When we find ourselves in challenging times, we can first choose to see the situations from different perspectives as we play them back in our minds. We can then decide which perspective will do us the most good: to hold on to what feeds our sense of injustice, to fuel our anger, or to chill a bit, knowing "this too shall pass." Instant Replay. We all have it. Whether it is a curse or a blessing depends on how many cameras we are using. We give meaning to whatever occurs.

Steps for Deeper Understanding

Where are you feeling some insistence or resistance today?

Try to look at your circumstance from a different perspective, perhaps one you suspect another person might have if placed in a similar situation.

Choose, if even for a short time, to let go of thoughts and feelings that make you right and another person wrong.

Notes:_____

_____

_____

_____

DAY 11: FORWARD MOMENTUM

Are you making progress? Are you able to look at your life and say, with certainty, that you are moving forward and not backward? It is the nature of the universe to move forward; we are all in a process of evolution. The word evolution comes from Latin, meaning "unrolling." Evolution is a kind of opening up to what we are becoming.

Yet in this process of unrolling, of evolution, of becoming, we sometimes think we are moving backward. You've heard the phrase "three steps forward, and two steps back." However, even with its fits and starts, life is moving forward.

We may be facing challenges on the job, with a tough boss or difficult co-workers. Maybe we have a serious problem with one or more of our relationships. Many people will need to deal with health issues from time to time. Depending on how we choose to frame these situations, they are not setbacks, but ways forward. Moving into and through our challenges is forward momentum. Even in our troubles, growth happens. *We never become <u>less experienced.</u>* Instead, we learn along the way.

Have you found yourself facing the same, or at least similar, issues over and over? You can't pay xyz *again* or you are dealing with heartbreak in your close relationship *again.*

Whatever we have learned in life to this point, we learned the first time through, or we had the opportunities to learn from repeated experiences. We always have the opportunity for a course correction. As soon as we muster the courage to do what we know we need to do, change occurs. As soon as we truly commit to a positive change, life supports us in that change.

W.H. Murray tells us in *The Scottish Himalayan Expedition:* "This may sound too simple, but is great in consequence. Until one is committed, there is hesitancy, the chance to draw back, always ineffectiveness. Concerning all acts of initiative (and creation), there is one elementary truth the ignorance of which kills countless ideas and splendid plans: that the moment one definitely commits oneself, then providence moves too. A whole stream of events issues from the decision, raising in one's favor all manner of unforeseen incidents, meetings and material assistance, which no man could have dreamt would have come his way. I learned a deep respect for one of Goethe's couplets: Whatever you can do or dream you can, begin it. Boldness has genius, power and magic in it!"

If you have ever driven a stick shift car, you must depress the clutch at the moment you shift gears. During that moment, the forward acceleration is slightly hampered. You are still moving forward, but no increasing power happens in that moment. You are not stalled. You are not stopped. You are still moving, just not accelerating.

That moment of non-acceleration happens in life, as well. When we shift gears (or jobs or interests), we may feel like we are temporarily losing power; but we are not stopped. We are just moving into another gear.

Sometimes we need to not only shift gears, but also change direction. If we have been going in the wrong direction, we see the results. We may feel a bit lost. I have heard someone say that when you go so far down, you reach a point at which changing direction and changing your life hurts less than continuing in the downward spiral you have created. But, in truth, we do not need to hit bottom before moving back up. Whenever we see the need for change in our lives, we can make a new commitment to ourselves. When we make a full commitment, then, as Murray states, providence moves, too. We do have help in the form of unforeseen advocates, brilliant ideas, and unexpected aid. We need only hold to our commitment and our faith. I like to say, "There is not a downside to looking up!"

A minister friend once had his congregation adopt this affirmation: "There is a power within us that is always greater than the condition before us." His congregation went from $200,000 in the red to $2.4 million in the bank. Each person had the chance to personalize that affirmation: "There is a power within me that is always greater than the condition before me." The congregation trusted in the higher power within them, collectively and individually. Their faith brought results.

Sometimes we find ourselves in chaos or feeling desperate about some aspect of our life. We must remember, always, that we are never alone. We are spiritual beings as well as human beings, and we are intimately connected to something greater. Let us hold to our faith, our belief that we are indeed making progress, despite appearances. Remember to hold on to an optimistic faith and look for tangible results.

Steps for Deeper Understanding

Do you feel like you are truly making progress, or are you just moving through life?

To what can you be committed, today? What can make you feel better tomorrow about what you did today?

Remind yourself: There is a power within me that is always greater than the condition before me!

Notes:_____

_____

_____

_____

DAY 12: CALLED HIGHER

We are being called higher — each of us, now, today. We are being called to be all that we came here to be.

I believe most of us are open to a deeper understanding of life, and we desire to have a more spiritual experience. Moses certainly had a spiritual experience, as we read in the third chapter of Exodus, where he approaches the burning bush and hears the voice of God: "... you shall say to the Israelites 'I am has sent me to you.'" *I am* is identified as the name of God.

We may read that scripture as though it is about ourselves. We use the term "I am" quite frequently. As we do, in a certain sense, we are invoking God.

Here it helps to notice *how* we say what we say. When we say, "I am tired" or "I am angry" or "I am sick" we charge that phrase with God-energy. We need to remember that's not who we *are*; that's how we *feel*. I don't want to affirm "I am" anything that I don't want to be.

Additionally, the Hebrew word used for "I am" is *hayah* [pronounced "haw-yah"], also translated as "becoming." I like to think I am continually growing. I am becoming what I am becoming.

We are always in the process of becoming more than we were. We learn, through study and experience. We are becoming what and who we were created to be. How do we do that? We can remember that we are spiritual beings, living in a spiritual universe governed by spiritual law. We can practice seeing beyond the obvious.

Jesus saw beyond the obvious. Otherwise, how could he even attempt to feed more than five thousand people with a few loaves of bread and a couple of fish? But Jesus gave thanks for what he had, which proved to be more than enough.

Jesus saw beyond the obvious when he saw wellness instead of illness in others, such as the paralytic at Bethesda. He helped those people see that quality in themselves, too, adding, "Your faith has made you well."

As we see, so it is. What would you prefer to see? Author Jack Canfield once described his mentor W. Clement Stone as an "inverse paranoid" who was convinced that the world was out to do him good: Everything that happened was destined to instantly or eventually benefit him. As he saw, so it was for W. Clement Stone.

Anais Nis wrote that "we see things not as they are, but as we are." We help create our reality through our perspective.

Additionally, definition is a prerequisite for resolution. When we define a situation, we begin to take charge of it. It no longer controls us. Rather than exaggerate or amplify the situation with worry or what-ifs, we just need to define it. Simply put, "This is so. So what?"

If we are facing a challenge, if we have some doubt or confusion, let us choose to see it differently. We go through phases of experience and understanding. We move from confusion to celebration.

We choose to release the assumptions we have made throughout our lives, realizing that at least sometimes they have limited us. Instead, we see beyond appearances, beyond the obvious. We use our gifts of faith and imagination. We open to new solutions, to insights and inspirations, to what we might call "divine ideas."

From there we move into incubation. Spiritual understanding requires letting go of preconceived ideas, the need to figure it all out, and the need to control or have it "our way." Only then can we truly open ourselves up to transformation, to illumination. That illumination may come to us in a flash or like a slow dawning. But when it happens, we see from a new perspective, and we are changed in the process.

Finally we move into the celebration phase. We have proven that our prayers and our principles do indeed work.

We need only remember to move through the phases —confusion, exploration, incubation, illumination, and then celebration —at the speed of spirit. See beyond the obvious, feel the activity of spirit, and experience God in your life. You are being called higher, to become all you came here to be.

The
WITCH
of
ENDOR

The
WITCH
of
ENDOR

SORCERESS *or* GODDESS

CAROLE LUNDE

THE WITCH OF ENDOR
SORCERESS OR GODDESS

Scripture quotations marked KJV are from the Holy Bible, King James Version (Authorized Version). First published in 1611. Quoted from the KJV Classic Reference Bible, Copyright © 1983 by The Zondervan Corporation.

iUniverse books may be ordered through booksellers or by contacting:

iUniverse
1663 Liberty Drive
Bloomington, IN 47403
www.iuniverse.com
1-800-Authors (1-800-288-4677)

ISBN: 978-1-5320-9945-8 (sc)
ISBN: 978-1-5320-9946-5 (e)

Library of Congress Control Number: 2020907448

Print information available on the last page.

iUniverse rev. date: 04/23/2020

INTRODUCTION

In the Hebrew Testament there is nothing about this woman's life save the interaction with King Saul. So questions arise. Who could she have been? Where did she come from or was she a native of the Village Endor? If she had such powers, how did she avoid being imprisoned, killed, or driven out of the land?

In the Book of Exodus the law is stated as, "You shall not permit a sorceress to live." This indicates that it would be a woman.

But in the Book of Deuteronomy it is decreed that "anyone who practices divination, a soothsayer, or an augur, or a sorcerer, a medium, a wizard, or a necromancer, you shall drive them out before you." Anyone is indicating man or woman, not necessarily to be killed, but driven away.

The "Witch" of Endor is a modern designation or label for this woman, but the word witch is not used in the Bible. Sorceress or medium or a woman with a familiar spirit are the terms.

Some rulers were diligent about this decree and some were not. However King Saul was one who was observant regarding this law, having his guards search them out, mostly because he was afraid of the anger of God if he did not.

King Saul asked the servants to find a woman who had "a familiar spirit" indicating a medium. King Saul's servants seemed to know such a woman and where she could be found. He demanded of his terrified servants to be taken to her.

This woman of Endor had not been officially accused of being a sorceress, but whatever the servants knew, she was sought out as if she might be one. Since this passage states the woman made a loud cry in fear when she saw something rise, some interpreters reject the suggestion that the woman was responsible for summoning Samuel's spirit because the indications are that this was an extraordinary event for her and a frightening one. She thought it was an evil foreign god of some kind, but it was actually Saul alone who declared that it was Samuel.

Another anomaly of that time was the popularity of the goddess, Astarte. The Phoenicians regarded this as most beneficial to their prosperity, and consequently the prosperity of the land of Judah, Lebanon, and Assyria. So it appears that the Jews welcomed and the worshipped this goddess along with Yahweh. Altars to Yahweh and the Asherahs of Astarte stood side by side in many places.

The Hebrew Testament was written as saga or story, not necessarily as chronological history although it is based on historical events, backgrounds, and people. It is full of stories written to tell the people what God would do for them if they were faithful and what God would do to them if they were disobedient.

These stories were written 1000 to 4000 years ago, many taken from even earlier cultures. They came from a completely different civilization from ours, the ancient Middle Eastern world, and not written for the modern western world. We may not understand their symbolism, but we can understand lessons in those stories relevant to our own lives.

We are given much information about those early cultures and can orient or place ourselves in the situations with questions. What would I have felt? What would I have said? What would have been important to me? Even though we cannot actually be there, we can create our own experience in regard to what is presented in the stories and enjoy having it be part of us. We identify with them in the same way that we identify with characters in novels and movies.

The Bible is called the Book of Life because it contains everything that can happen to humanity. Nothing is left out. "The thing that has been, it is that which shall be; and that which is done is that which shall be done; and there is no new thing under the sun." (Ecclesiastes 1:9)KJV

Each character in the stories is actually a reflection of some part of us. So, in engaging the stories, we can actually explore the many facets of ourselves.

I invite you to come on an adventure with me as we answer some questions about who this woman might have been and what might the many episodes of her life have been that brought her to the place where she shows up in 1 Samuel 28:3 through 25.

CHAPTER 1

Majah was the High Priestess in the Temple of Astarte. She was a striking woman. She was diminutive with snapping dark eyes, light skin, long black hair, and the regal bearing one would expect of a true High Priestess.

She grew up in the temple and became one of the most proficient in the cosmic arts. Her innate knowledge of the movement of the planets and cosmic energies was unsurpassed. Aligned with her high accomplishment in these things, she was also kind, loving and caring of all who needed her instruction and help.

Her deep understanding and openness made her vulnerable to the darkening realm of Ba'al, which was far from kind and caring. Astarte and Ba'al were said to be consorts much like the yin and yang, or the light and dark side of the forces. Lately, the dark side was constantly calling to Majah disturbing her dreams at night with strange dark images. There was something new in its energy, evil.

Puzzled and frustrated, she decided to quiet that disturbance once and for all by going to the Temple of Ba'al to learn what she could about the origin of these dark images and why she was plagued by them.

Abigail was a senior student and friend of Majah. She was of Phoenician descent, a tall woman with long flowing silvery hair and light eyes. She was shocked at this turn of events and begged Majah not to give into the darkness.

"Please, mistress, it is so dangerous. No priestess of Astarte has ever gone to the Temple of Ba'al! Is there not another way to overcome this?"

"If this is part of me, then I must know more about what it is and how to understand myself in regard to it. Being the High Priestess of the light is wonderful, but I keep thinking there might be even more that is calling to me.

"It is from the darkness where the power comes from and secrets lie in its mystery. Surely this is somehow part of the great cosmic God over all, for nothing else can exist."

Abigail was terrified for Majah. The Temple of Astarte had always been about light, not about darkness.

"Will you take someone with you to protect you?"

"No, that would not be wise. I cannot endanger someone else. When I create the Secret Way for myself alone, no one else can enter it. It will be my protector. Please, Abigail, be calm and help me prepare."

They went to the garden spot where the vespers were held and spent long hours in meditation together. As they walked out of the garden at the music summoning them to a meal, Majah was frowning.

"Mistress, has anything changed since the meditation?"

"Yes it has. It is as if the calling is stronger. I must go to Rébekah at Endor to consult with her and test the energies. I want to understand all I need to know and do before I make the journey to the Temple of Ba'al. Please come with me."

"Of course I will come with you. Who is Rébekah, Majah?"

"Rébekah is a widow woman of Endor. Her husband, Adaiah, was a priest of Ba'al. She was a priestess of the Temple of Astarte. They were in love and when they saw that the Temple of Ba'al was becoming dark and evil, she went to help him free himself.

"The evil High Priest of Ba'al tried to trap them, promising them a marriage ceremony to unite them. As soon as the ceremony was concluded they gathered all the powers of the cosmos to aid them and they escaped."

"And they went to Endor?"

"Yes. This meant that they must stay forever in the forests and cliffs above Endor where they could live in peace. They devoted themselves to doing many good works for the people and were dearly loved by them. The High Priest of Ba'al sent word that they were sorcerers and should be found, not be allowed to live, but the people of the Village of Endor knew this was not true. They shielded and protected them.

"What happened to her husband?"

"He was forced to use much his energy to keep the darkness at bay. It seems that the priesthood vows he took gave the darkness a permanent hook into his mind or spirit that could not be broken, only blocked. Rébekah helped him all that she could with her own energy, which enabled him to live much longer than he might have.

"The darkness held evil and was relentless. It tore at him in the night. The Temple of Astarte covered him with a powerful divine light but it was not enough to completely free him. When he eventually died the Temple light enabled his soul to remain free in the eternal light. The evil darkness could not follow him there."

"How sad! It makes me want to cry."

"Rébekah was almost inconsolable, but the village and the priestesses took care of her through her terrible grief. Now the village continues to protect her for the rest of her life. Some elderly priestesses volunteered to live the remainder of their lives in the Village of Endor. They hold the light to ensure the Temple's continued safety and Rébekah's wellbeing to this day."

After their dinner time, Abigail and Majah went back to the garden at twilight and sat down to focus their minds on Endor. Majah created the Secret Way for both of them and immediately they were in Endor, high on the cliffs of the mountains.

Rébekah came out of her hut and threw her arms open to them.

"Welcome, Majah and you must be Abigail! What troubles you that you come to me? Come and sit down. I have some wine and bread to refresh you."

Abigail was fascinated to see her. Rébekah had long white hair something like her own, but browned skin that made her face look like wrinkled parchment. Her eyes were piercing but kind, and her nearly toothless smile was merry. It was impossible to tell how old she was, but she had the appearance of a wizened one who had lived long and understood much.

"Majah, my daughter, you look very disturbed."

True, she only nibbled at the bread and drank a small portion of wine quickly.

"I did not wish to bring this to you, but there is a dark evil energy that I am sure comes from the Temple of Ba'al. It disturbs my dreams with dark images that draw me toward them. It becomes more intense as time goes on. I believe I must go to Ba'al's temple to understand what it is and how to stop it, or keep it under control before it endangers our priestesses and consumes my entire life!"

"Yes, it is good that you have come to me. Let me see…"

Rébekah closed her eyes and was quiet for several minutes. It was as if she entered a trance.

Then Abigail realized that Rébekah had created a Secret Way and they moved to a circle of benches surrounded by tall trees and yet was open to a great expanse of the sky. The stars were brighter than she had ever seen before and seemed to twinkle as if they knew she were there. A shiver ran through her that abruptly stopped when Rébekah began to speak.

"You must surely realize, Majah, that the power will be much stronger the closer you get to the temple. If you enter, it will engulf you. You have much power of your own, but if the dream images are so strong as to draw you, you may not be strong enough to free yourself when you are actually in the Temple of Ba'al itself and standing before these images."

"Are you saying that I should not go?"

"I cannot tell you not to go, although I would like to have that power. You must decide. But if you go, you must construct the Secret Way so that it is always attached to your body as well as your mind, and will retrieve you upon command. That command must be so embedded in your mind and heart that you can access it immediately and soundlessly no matter what is happening around you."

"So I cannot just walk out at will, but I will be forcibly detained?"

"Yes, that is exactly what I am saying. Adaiah and I planned carefully to join our energy forces in the ceremony and to escape at the end of a ceremony just before another event could begin. It was a weak spot that was momentary. It would open and close in an instant and we slipped through in that instant."

CHAPTER 2

Why are we not as powerful as the High Priest of Ba'al? Is a priestess less powerful?"

"It is an illusion perpetrated by the High Priest of Ba'al. A fly looks so much larger and stronger than a spider web, yet it cannot free itself. It has been inflicted with a poison and paralyzed."

"How would this poison be inflicted at the Temple of Ba'al?"

"The High Priest will try to seduce you and you must not let that happen! The love of Astarte and Ba'al is not physical. Being consorts does not mean knowing each other physically. It is two halves of a whole in which neither can overpower the other. However if evil is involved, the darkness will always try to overpower the light with deception, but it cannot. If it could do that, all worldly existence would be forever plunged into darkness and cease to exist."

"How can I stop the darkness from entering my dreams? Is there another way?"

"You are very open to the cosmos, Majah. You have gained much knowledge and skill. But now you must close that door before sleeping. Open it only when the morning light comes from the east."

"But I have always been available day and night when my work is needed. If I close that door…"

Abigail suddenly interjected.

"I can hold that door open for you, Majah! I can learn how. I will awaken you if you are summoned."

Rébekah was silent and closed her eyes. After a few minutes she took a deep breath and began to speak.

"Before you decide anything, stay here with me tonight and I will keep watch over you. I want to know exactly what these images are, how and when they come to you. If you decide to try Abigail's suggestion and Abigail is not skilled enough or the darkness overpowers her and breaks through to you, you must stop immediately. But of course that will create a weak moment and the shift may not be quick enough. Perhaps it is better that we think of something else."

They went back to Rébekah's roomy hut and lay down exhausted. Majah felt safe for the first time in several years. Sometime in the night when Majah began tossing and turning, Rébekah shook her awake.

"What did it look like, Majah?"

"It took the form of a strange black statue, an animal I have never seen before. I do not know what animal it is."

"Ah! I do know what it is! It is among several black statues of strange animals in the garden of Ba'al's temple. The High Priest cannot use his own image because he cannot control an image of himself while he is producing it, so he uses something else to frighten and weaken you."

"So if the animal has no power, it is Ba'al's power?"

"Likely his High Priest who openly worships an image of Ba'al where people can see him. He makes his priests believe that he has the full power of Ba'al."

"What can I do against this?"

"Close the cosmic door of your mind at night, Majah. Others must be told that you are not to be disturbed in the night. Do not use Abigail to keep the door open. She will not be strong enough if the High Priest recognizes her and attacks her. He will try to destroy her and get to you. It is not safe."

"It seems there is nothing I can do but sacrifice myself to this and then perhaps he will leave everyone else alone."

"That is foolishness, Majah. Your sacrifice will open the door and give him free access to the Temple of Astarte. He will continue to attack any High Priestess of Astarte because you all carry the light. He will seek to destroy what he cannot have."

They broke their fast together at a morning meal and were very quiet. They walked in the woods together, each one contemplating her part in this dark drama.

"I wish you could stay with me forever, Majah, but I know it is not possible. The evil part of the darkness never completely let go of Adaiah."

They returned to the hut and hugged each other.

"Abigail and I shall return to the Temple of Astarte and I will concentrate on what my path will be. There must be a way to maintain a balance so that we are not constantly under attack from this dark power. We have survived so long without a problem and I must do what I can."

Rébekah gave them a special blessing before they left.

"The Temple of Astarte has survived for thousands of years without interference because there has not been a priestess with your level of cosmic understanding. This understanding came to you from many years of strengthening light. You are a vessel of the light. Now the darkness desires that power and seeks to destroy you to get it. I will cover you with the light of Astarte and will remain in meditation until you safely return."

Majah and Abigail went back to the Temple of Astarte somewhat saddened that there was no clear answer except for Majah to stay at the Temple and contend with the dark nightmares, or go to the Temple of Ba'al.

She concentrated on closing the cosmic door to her mind as she went to bed. She was so accustomed to openness that it seemed to be a darkness that was almost worse than the nightmares. She felt totally helpless without the cosmic connection and would awaken in the morning feeling exhausted and confused.

Abigail was worried watching Majah go through her rituals and duties every day as if in a fog. She spoke little and ate almost nothing. Abigail joined her at the altar of flowers.

"We will pray to Astarte for help!"

"I would rather do face to face battle with Ba'al than to live like this! I am in darkness all the time! Who can be a High Priestess of Astarte if she lives in darkness?"

7

She went to sleep that night without closing her mind and the dark images came stronger than before. She thrashed about and called out in her sleep. Abigail came quickly to her bedside.

"Mistress, I am here. Wake up!"

Majah sat up with a start and Abigail threw her arms around her.

"Oh, Mistress, was it even worse?"

"Yes! Now I know what I must do if I want my life and my light back. I will not sit here helpless and let it be taken from me."

She arose from her bed, wrapped a heavy robe around her shoulders, pulled up the hood, and went to the vesper place in the garden to kneel at the altar of light and flowers. She lit a candle and focused on the light.

"Great and glorious Astarte, hear my prayer. Guide me and be with me as I go to the Temple of Ba'al to discover the evil source of my dark dreams. I must stop them before they threaten us all forever. Bless me with strength to break the path of the dark energy to your temple and vanquish it."

Abigail met Majah at the vesper garden.

"You are going, are you not?"

"Yes, I must."

CHAPTER 3

"May I go with you?"

"Beloved Abigail, you must stay here should I not come back. I will create the Secret Way, attach it to my body as Rébekah said, with a command that will return me instantly to this place. I will stay open to the light no matter what happens. Let Ba'al's priest do his worst. I will not be taken!"

"And the light will not fail you, Majah. I will keep a vigil of light here for your success and safe return."

They hugged and Majah went to work in her mind creating the Secret Way and its attachment to her body. She had never created this kind of attachment before and it was a little more difficult. She had to be sure every molecule of her physical body was within it and held secure.

Eventually she succeeded in placing an anchoring signal that would immediately activate it. She knew that it must not unravel, but hold tight in the most extreme situations.

When she was sure it was secure she aimed it toward the Temple of Ba'al. She stepped into the Secret Way and immediately she stood in the desert before the gate of the darkened temple.

The place was huge and forbidding. The stones of the façade were dark and jagged from years of misuse of the power by the High Priest. A priest dressed in a black robe, carrying a torch, stepped forth from the temple gate and greeted her by name.

"Welcome, High Priestess Majah! We have been expecting you. Please come in. We have prepared a meal for you and comfortable quarters."

Majah could sense the darkness closing around her. It was cold, or at least it made her feel chilled. Head held high she followed the priest to the rooms supposedly prepared for her. She was sure it was all a ploy to get her to lower her guard and be vulnerable.

"The High Priest will see you this evening."

"I prefer to see him in the daylight."

"He is away and will not return until late evening. Please make yourself comfortable."

Then the imperious priest abruptly walked away and disappeared in the myriad of intersecting hallways. Majah looked at the food. She was suspicious of it. Not really hungry anyway she decided to sustain her body with the light. She lifted its vibration high above the need for physical sustenance.

The priest returned late that afternoon to check on her, entering her room without a knock.

"Your food has not been touched. Why have you not eaten? Would you like me to bring you something else if this is not to your liking?"

Majah rounded on him and caught him by surprise.

"Why is your dark energy targeting me? What are these strange black animals that come into my dreams? What do you and the High Priest hope to accomplish?"

"The High Priest will answer your questions when he arrives."

Abruptly he turned and walked out.

Majah wandered down a hall and out into a garden, or what may have been a garden at one time. But now it was a courtyard full of stones and black statues of strange animals. Now she was sure the attacks were coming from this place. As the skies darkened, she turned to go back to her rooms when the High Priest loomed before her.

"Do you like my garden, Majah?"

Majah blazed in anger at this abrupt intrusion. He was high handed and imperious and she hated him immediately.

"What do you want? Why are you targeting me?"

"My dear you must know that you are a worthy mate and we should perform the love rituals of Astarte and Ba'al to insure the prosperity of the land and its people. This is our duty! I will come to your room tonight and we will begin."

Majah tried to access the Secret Way, but felt somehow blocked. She was sure it must be the High Priest. Trying not to panic she turned and walked steadily back to her room to refocus her mind and concentrate.

"Astarte keep me strong. Astarte keep me focused. I must escape now!"

The priest arrived at her door to announce that the High Priest was on his way and she should prepare. He placed a black robe on her chair by the door and hesitated, turning to look her up and down before he walked away. In that moment of hesitation he stood between Majah and the energy of the High Priest. Majah issued the command to the Secret Way and she was swept away to the vesper garden where Abigail was waiting.

"Majah! All thanks to Astarte that you have returned! Are you all right? What happened?"

"We must go to Rébekah immediately. I must tell her what I saw and felt."

"Yes, of course, but first let us have some food. You look like you are about to faint!"

"I suppose I do look pale. It was as if the energy were being sucked out of me. I ate nothing while there, fearful that it might be poisoned in some way that would paralyze me as the spider paralyzes the fly. I am thankful for my command that worked instantly and took no energy to invoke, because I had none left."

Rébekah was in her garden when Majah and Abigail arrived.

"You went there! I can see it in your aura. It looks a bit depleted with dark places in it. All thanks to Astarte that you escaped! Come in, sit down and tell me everything that happened."

Majah described the place, the dark energy, the stone garden with its black statues, and the haughty forbidding High Priest.

"The High Priest called me a worthy mate to perform the rituals that would consummate the love of Astarte and Ba'al. I could not summon the Secret Way in his presence. I went back to my rooms and the priest brought me a black robe to wear. In the moment he hesitated at my door, he must have broken the energy flow between the High Priest and me, and I issued the command that brought me instantly back to our vesper place."

"What have you learned from this experience, Majah?"

"I learned to prepare well and not to interface directly with that evil dark energy. It must be interrupted or deflected in some way so it cannot trap me."

"Very good, my dear. This is not a final lesson, but it is a major step in your ability to work in the cosmic light. Of course I would suggest that you not return to the Temple of Ba'al ever again. Once in that darkness is enough. Stay here tonight and we will see if you have succeeded in deterring the attacks."

Abigail and Majah were wakeful for a few hours and chatted quietly so as not to disturb Rébekah. They eventually drifted off to sleep, and Majah slept undisturbed for the rest of the night. They awakened early and Majah felt energized and full of light.

Overjoyed, she and Abigail splashed cool water on their faces, neck, and arms and patted themselves dry. They went into the kitchen and sat down near the hearth where Rébekah was preparing food for the day.

"You had a peaceful night, Majah?"

"Yes, very peaceful and full of sweet dreams filled with light. I am rested and feel like myself again. Rébekah, do you think I am free, at least for now?"

"Yes, you are, but none of us is free forever. We must still be vigilant, but I would say you have confronted the monster and lived to tell about it. If you would like to stay a few more days and regain your strength, you are of course welcome."

Majah wanted to stay forever in this beloved place where she felt so safe.

"I think we have much work to do at the Temple of Astarte and should be there now. The young priestesses will be waiting for us. But Abigail, would you like to stay here and talk further with Rébekah?"

"Yes, I would and this place is lovely and peaceful, but I must return with you, Majah. We are bound together in this work and should remain so. Thank you, Rébekah."

Rébekah hugged them both and kissed their cheeks.

"Go in light and peace, my dear ones. Return to me when it is right."

CHAPTER 4

King Saul's men went about the countryside tearing down the Asherah poles that stood next to the altars of Yahweh, as declared in the laws of Deuteronomy. He regularly sent his guards to find the poles because someone would always put them up again. They were to arrest any woman accused of being a sorceress or who "had a spirit," as they called it.

He had heard of the great beauty of the women at the Temple of Astarte and the many blessings they brought to the land. The Phoenicians brought a lucrative sea trade for the kingdom, especially purple dyes for the royalty, and Astarte was their beneficent Goddess. They were never considered to do sorcery of any kind.

King Saul could not go to their temple to view them so he decided to issue an invitation, a summons to Majah, the High Priestess, to come to his fortress in Gibeah for a banquet in honor of Astarte.

Majah was puzzled at this invitation. This had never happened before. His god was Yahweh. Why would he honor Astarte?

"Mistress, what will you do? We do not have anything to do with King Saul or Israel at the level of royalty. This is not who we are!"

"I fear it might be a trap, but we cannot afford to insult the king by refusing. He might send his troops to our temple. Perhaps I can delay this meeting. I will have a message taken to King Saul thanking him for his invitation, but I am not well and cannot come at this time."

"But we have no illnesses among us!"

"True, but I trust he does not know that."

Majah knew that Samuel the prophet would greatly disapprove.

"Also, I will send a message to Samuel through the shepherds in the fields to notify him of this strange invitation. Hopefully, he will respond and advise King Saul not to disturb our temple."

When Majah's message came to Samuel he shook his head in disgust.

"Saul, Saul, what are you doing now? This will surely not please God! Do you not know that by now, or do you just never think at all! When will you think about God first before you do something?"

Picking up his robe and staff, he went immediately to Gibeah, to King Saul. Saul was smiling over a servant girl and toying with her hair when Samuel came in angrily pounding his staff on the floor as he walked. Saul jolted upright.

"Samuel! What has happened? Have you heard something from God?"

"What are you doing ordering a High Priestess to come here? How dare you summon the High Priestess and violate the Temple of Astarte. You cannot give a banquet in Astarte's honor! The Lord God will not forgive you for this trespass! And what can you possibly want from the High Priestess? She is not available for the pleasure of men!"

Saul was taken aback by Samuel's rage. He paced around the room and stammered.

"H – How did you now? I was just curious. We never see them. How do we know they are not our enemies? Sorceresses casting spells on us? I must protect Israel!"

"I will tell you who your enemies are and are not! You will wait until God speaks to you or to me, and you will not do anything else so foolish."

"But am I not the king? I can order whatever I want!"

"You are king only so long as you please God, who chose you!"

Samuel was livid. He had been praying every day that God would take this wild unruly man off his hands and off the throne. Saul always stumbled and failed when he was not following God, and was victorious when he obeyed God's word through Samuel. But Saul could not see that. He was driven by emotions, fears, and superstitions.

Saul turned to the doorway and shouted for his guard, Malachi.

"Sire, may I serve you in some way?"

14

"Yes! Send a message to the Temple of Astarte that the invitation I sent to the High Priestess is rescinded!"

"Yes, Sire, immediately!"

Malachi bowed, backed out the door, and went to the servants' quarters to get a messenger and gave him explicit instructions.

"Take one of Saul's asses and ride fast. Deliver this message to the Temple of Astarte and come back immediately to tell me it is done!"

Asses were a very fast and beautiful animal, and highly prized by royalty and the wealthy. They had belonged to Saul's wealthy father, Kish, a Benjaminite. The servant's eyebrows shot up at the mention of Saul's favorite animals, but nodded and ran toward the stable.

Samuel waited impatiently for Malachi's return to declare that the deed was done. When Malachi finally returned, Samuel noted that Malachi was also getting on in years because he bowed stiffly and backed more slowly out of Saul's presence. Then Samuel, not looking at Saul again, turned to depart as well.

As Samuel pounded his walking stick and vehemently strode away, Saul cried out and fell on his face grabbing at Samuel's robe and it tore. Samuel looked down in disgust at Saul groveling on the floor.

"Because of your disobedience the Lord has torn away the Kingdom of Israel from you!"

Samuel walked on out and Saul got up looking around to see if anyone witnessed his shame. Somewhat relieved that he was alone, he ran out to the encampment to be with his troops which always made him feel powerful again.

Majah was both thankful and puzzled when Saul's message came from the fortress of Gibeah and was delivered to the temple. The messenger declined their hospitality or even refreshment, and rode away as fast as he had arrived.

"What can this mean, mistress? The summons is rescinded. Have we done something to anger the king? Are we in danger?"

"I believe that Samuel went to Saul and chastised him for intending to violate the sanctity of the Temple of Astarte. So we are free of this for now. Also we have always been protected by the Phoenicians and honored by the people of this land. They know we bring only good."

Majah laughed and hugged Abigail. They walked into the garden together to enjoy its beautiful flowers.

"But we might still be in danger, might we not? It is all so sudden. Do you think Ba'al has gotten to the king as well? His darkness is everywhere. I hear Saul is quite erratic in his behavior, strange and demonical, fierce and threatening."

"We must be watchful, Abigail, but we must not fear. To be fearful is to forget the love of Astarte. That is the danger."

In the late evening Majah was walking through the temple garden and past the gate. She saw a movement outside the gate and went out to see what it was, thinking it was a messenger or someone who needed help.

A man in a dark cloak grabbed her, pressed his hand to her mouth, and dragged her away to a waiting chariot. Her hands were bound with a cord and a blindfold was placed over her eyes. She struggled but to no avail. The hands that held her were like iron. No one said a word to her. After what seemed like a very long time, the chariot stopped and she was carried into an abandoned stable and deposited on the straw on the floor.

"Who are you? What do you want? I am a High Priestess!"

The blindfold was taken off and a tall man with wild eyes stood over her. He removed his tunic exposing his nakedness and lay down upon her, pulling her robe aside.

"You must not do this! It is an abomination!"

Roughly he forced himself into her and she screamed. The pain was excruciating and she cried out for him to stop, but he did not. He tore at her body over and over. When he was spent, the men picked her up, put her back into the chariot, and dumped her at the gate of the Temple of Astarte.

Crying, bruised and bleeding, Majah crawled to the gate and screamed for help. Abigail and two other priestesses came running to the gate.

CHAPTER 5

"Majah, is that you? Great Astarte, what happened?"

They picked her up and carried her into her quarters where she fainted.

"Call a midwife immediately!"

One was summoned to examine and tend to her injuries.

"She has been brutally raped. There is much tearing. She should keep very still to heal or she might bleed to death."

Abigail almost collapsed in shock.

"But who could have done this?"

"I do not know. She will have to tell you that herself."

Majah was badly shaken and spent months alone, slowly healing and not speaking to anyone. Abigail sat with her day after day, tending to her, feeding her, bathing her, and sharing her silence. Majah's belly began to swell and it was clear that she was with child.

Saul knew that Majah would not recognize him, or so he hoped. He busied himself with his troops preparing for the attack from the Philistines. What happened to the High Priestess was a scandal and word came to him that the High Priestess was pregnant. He became frantic and paced back and forth.

"Samuel must not hear of this! He will realize it was me. He will know what I have done to the High Priestess."

Saul hurried to declare her a sorceress and claimed that she cast a spell on him. He sent his soldiers to quietly take her from the temple garden in the night and bring her to the prison. Now he could legally imprison and have her killed. No one would know.

Everyone in the Temple of Astarte was in shock. They wandered about the temple, numbly doing their tasks, hardly speaking. Majah was gone for the second time and no one knew how it happened or where she was.

Malachi, head servant of King Saul, was standing guard by Majah's cell. He was incensed. Anyone could have gotten to Majah. There were no guards at the Temple. None were ever needed. No one would think of violating the Temple of Astarte or her High Priestess. Only one person he could think of would do such a thing. King Saul.

An envoy of the king imperiously arrived and accosted Malachi.

"I am here to witness that the sorceress is dead and report back to the king! When will she be dead?"

"The woman is already in prison! What is the hurry? What are you afraid of? Do you think she will put a spell on you? Maybe she will! You had better go far away tonight before she gets to your soul and steals it!"

Slightly shaken Aphiah took a deep breath and stated it more emphatically.

"The law requires that she should be burned or stoned to death, I do not care which you do, but kill her! We shall not suffer a sorceress to live! It is the law!"

"It shall be done in the early morning. Do you wish to witness this terrible sight? Have you ever seen a sorceress stoned or burned? Her black soul will rise over you and haunt you for the rest of your life!"

The terrified envoy was shaking in his boots. He turned and departed immediately.

It was growing cold in the night. Malachi started a small fire in a grate to warm her chill damp cell a little. He spread a tattered robe on the filthy floor and gently moved her onto it closer to the fire.

"Majah, when will your child be born? Soon? We have arranged for a safe home where no one will know about the child."

"Soon, Malachi, she will come very soon. I feel the pains strengthening now. It will be a daughter. She is Ishtara, but that name will be hidden for many years."

As Majah screamed in pain, a small cry came forth out of the dark and filth of the dungeon. A daughter was born. Malachi eased the child out of Majah's body and tied off the umbilical cord. He wrapped her in clean swaddling clothes, to be immediately spirited away by a messenger the same night.

Malachi gave Majah a strong sleeping potion. Early the next morning she was dragged from her cell unconscious, taken to a deserted quarry, and stoned to death. Only the tears of Malachi and the small cry of an infant marked her passing.

"The law is fulfilled, my Lord."

The envoy bowed deeply and knelt before King Saul, keeping his frightened face turn away.

"You are sure? Absolutely? If she is not dead, you soon will be! I will cut off your head myself!"

"Yes, my Lord, I saw to it myself."

Aphiah had lied. He had not witnessed it. He could not imagine now he had gotten himself into this. He was honored to be chosen to serve the king and now he was most anxious to depart from Saul's threatening presence.

"Good. Here is your price. Take your leave of me and return to your home. You are sworn to silence upon pain of death. The matter is forever closed."

"Yes, my Lord. Forever closed."

Aphiah was shaking so much that he was not sure his legs lift him up.

"Get up and get out of my sight!"

Terror caused him to jump up and hurry away, remembering the warning of Malachi, that Majah could have put a spell on him. The hair began to stand up on the back of his neck and chills ran through his body. He broke into a run toward the stables, mounted his horse, paid the stable servant, and frantically galloped away through the streets of Gibeah.

The envoy, while hesitating at the city gate as it slowly opened, told a guard at the gate that Majah, the sorceress, had a female child. He did not know this for sure, but it would turn Saul's attention away from pursuing and murdering him.

Word was passed to the servants who told Saul and he went crazy. He began shouting and pacing, throwing urns and furniture, threatening everyone around him.

"Is the child alive? Where was she taken? Who is hiding her? You must find and do away with her, and everyone who has her! Kill them all! Kill them all!"

He was terrified every day and cried out in his nightmares when he slept. He was certain she would be a sorceress and that God was punishing him for his evil. She would surely cast dark spells upon him!

Ana and Tolah were anxiously waiting in a hidden cave to receive the child. The night seemed endless as they shivered over a tiny fire. Finally a hooded messenger appeared soundlessly, handed them the child, and quickly disappeared into the night.

They stamped out the fire and hurried home undetected while it was still dark. Once in their house Tolah lit a lamp. Ana eagerly opened the swaddling cloth to see an angelic face looking up at her. She had luminous skin, dark eyes and black hair. Her little fist found her mouth and she began to suck on it.

"Tolah, bring Puah quickly. She is the serving woman in the kitchen who just had a stillborn child. We need her to nurse the infant."

Puah came quickly and was puzzled as she peered into the tiny face.

"But whose child is this, my lady? Surely not yours."

"She is from my distant cousin who died in child birth. She was born on my knees and will be known as my child from now on."

"Yes, my lady. I understand. I am happy to care for her. Does she have a name?"

"Hodesha. That is her name."

"Hodesha, my lady? That name means….burning!"

"Yes, I know Puah. Just think of it as a burning bright light. She will be a bright light. And please be silent about the arrival of this child."

Nodding Puah gently lifted the infant from Ana's arms and carried her to the next room where she immediately began to nurse her.

"Hodesha! Hodesha the burning! Why a name like that? What could this mean?"

As Hodesha grew she remained diminutive, slightly built, and not particularly pretty or even noticeable. She was shy and kept her head down, but had penetrating dark eyes. She sat quietly as other kids romped and played. They thought her too small to join them.

"Ana, who is my mother? I know you are my mother, but who birthed me from her body?"

"Just a cousin who passed away, Hodesha. Someday I will tell you all about her, but not now."

"Someday I will be able to see her. I have dreams."

"We all have dreams, Hodesha. They come at night. I do not know how. Sometimes they are about real things in our lives and sometimes they are a mystery. Do your dreams frighten you?"

"Sometimes. But mostly I see people. I do not know them. But I know I will really see and meet them someday."

"How can you be sure?"

"I just know…I just know."

Ana was worried and admonished her to be silent about her dreams.

"You must not speak of this to anyone else. Promise me you will not."

"I will not. I promise."

Hodesha answered resolutely as if she somehow knew how important it was.

CHAPTER 6

As the years went by Hodesha grew more inward and kept to herself. Ana and Tolah became more and more aware that the town's people were gossiping and asking questions about little Hodesha.

"She is such a strange little child, Ana. Was your cousin strange as well?"

"She is not strange and her mother was a perfectly lovely person, kind as they come. I miss her very much and am proud to raise her child!"

The talk did not stop and Ana worried about Hodesha's safety.

"I fear, Tolah, that we must leave this place and go somewhere else to live. They are beginning to suspect that Hodesha's mother was a sorceress or that Hodesha is one."

"But she is not!"

"No, neither was her mother."

"But where do you think we should go? We may be hounded with questions wherever we are. The danger will follow us and we will be suspected because we are new to the next place."

"Tolah, she is a princess, not a sorceress. Perhaps it is time to take her to the Temple of Astarte where she will be protected and educated as a priestess of Astarte. She is almost twelve and will be with young girls like herself, not be ostracized or thought to be strange. It would please Majah."

"Yes, it would please Majah, but Hodesha must not make the mistakes that Majah made."

"Majah was under many pressures and influences. It was not her fault! Anyone can stumble when pursued by evil people."

"Yes, but it seems that being a High Priestess of the Temple of Astarte endangered and cost her life!"

"Come, Tolah! We must not think of that now or discuss it. We must gather our belongings and go."

Before dawn they set out on foot with one donkey to carry their bundles. The way to the temple was long, but they were carried swiftly by their sense of Hodesha's destiny. Hodesha was thrilled at the thought of becoming a priestess. It sounded wonderful even though she did not know what that would be like.

"But mother, I will miss you and father. Will I ever see you again? Where will you be? How will I find you if I need you?"

"You will be in training every day with many girls like you. You will be loved and well cared for. You will be very busy and learn to be a great priestess. We will always love you and pray to Astarte for your success and happiness. Do not worry. We will not forget you."

High on a hill sat an immense marble clad temple gleaming gold in the sun. The pathway up to it was a steep climb through many switch-backs. The closer they got, the larger it appeared until it seemed they were in another world.

There were beautiful flowering trees and gardens around it. The marble of the walls shimmered and there was music coming from within. The fragrance of the flowers floated all about. Hodesha was enchanted and in awe.

They stepped cautiously through a gate into a walled garden.

"Who are you and why are you here?"

The voice came from a woman at the edge of the garden. She had long silvery hair and was clothed in a light blue diaphanous robe and golden sandals.

Ana stepped forward holding Hodesha's hand.

"We have brought this child to be dedicated to Astarte. Her name is Hodesha, born of Majah."

"Who is Majah, mother?"

"She is your birth mother. Be silent for now."

"I am Abigail. You will please follow me."

She turned toward an ornate golden gate which opened immediately at her touch. Ana and Tolah with Hodesha between them followed her into a small anteroom.

Abigail, smiled warmly at Hodesha, looked her over carefully and asked a few questions.

"Are you willing to be devoted to the goddess, Astarte?"

"Yes."

Hodesha's voice was barely audible. She was still awed by her surroundings.

"Once you begin here, Hodesha, there is no turning back. You will not be able to return to Ana and Tolah. You will belong to the temple for the rest of your life. Do you understand this?"

"Yes, I do."

Hodesha was breathless and was sure she wanted to stay in this beautiful place forever.

"You will be obedient to all we tell you to do. You will comply without hesitation. Do you agree to this?"

"Yes, I will."

"Good. Do you have any questions?"

"Just one. Did you know my birth mother?"

"Yes, we knew her, but do not ask more. You will come to understand everything at the right time. That time is not now."

Hodesha nodded, a little disappointed, and fell silent.

Abigail turned to Ana and Tolah and smiled.

"We will accept her. You must leave now. Speak to no one of this day. Do not mention her name ever again. We will love and care for her. All will be well. Go with our blessing."

Ana and Tolah kissed Hodesha and bid her farewell. They were shown out through a different door into another room where they were given generous gifts that would sustain them for all of their years to come. They went carefully down a steep path that eventually joined the road at the bottom of the hill.

Ana fought back the tears. Something or someone whispered in her mind in a familiar voice.

"Thank you. You have done well. Accept my gifts and live in peace."

Tolah found their donkey, repacked it with the gifts, and they started on their way to find a new home and peace.

Abigail took Hodesha's hand. They walked through the lovely gardens, past the altar of Astarte and into the temple building. Hodesha was awed at everything she saw. She had been so quiet all her young life and now she was full of questions.

"Where is my room? Where will I live? Who will take care of me? What if no one likes me here? I do not know what to do and I am frightened that I will fail. What do I call you? Mother?"

"Be calm, Hodesha. You will have a room with another student priestess. We all take care of each other here and you will be taken care of, too. We are all devotees of Astarte and like her we love each other. There is no competition or judgement of each other, and no one fails. The only failure possible is if we fail to love each other and the benevolent goddess Astarte.

"You may call me Abigail. We are not mothers here, but your teachers and friends. You will learn that as time goes on. Do not worry about anything now."

Hodesha had much to think about as they continued to walk through the enormous temple, grounds, and bowers of flowers everywhere. She had never seen so many beautiful flowers of every color. Their scent enchanted her and seemed to surround her wherever she went.

CHAPTER 7

"Come child, you must be tired. You will have a lovely purification bath, a new tunic, and some rest. From now on your name will be Ishtara, no longer Hodesha."

"Ishtara? But why must my name be changed? I have always been Hodesha. My mother gave me this name."

"Your birth mother gave you the name Ishtara. You will learn more about her later when you are ready. Come with me now."

"I am right now Ishtara?"

"Yes. Hodesha does not exist anymore. You will never use or respond to that name. Do you understand?"

"What do I do if someone calls me by that name?"

"You will not react or respond in any way. You must pretend you do not hear that name. We will train you until you do not hear it. Do not be afraid."

Ishtara's bath was like nothing she had ever experienced in her young life. It was tepid and fragrant with flowers floating all around her. Young girls were there to massage her with fragrant oils. They washed and spilled fragrances into her hair. Then she was dried, wrapped in a soft warm robe, and led to a dressing area.

She was invited to lay down on a massage table and warm oil was rubbed into her skin. Then she was dried again and dressed in a short diaphanous tunic. It shimmered blue, purple, and silver when she walked around. Ishtara was completely enchanted.

They took her to a dimly lit room with several soft beds where she could rest. Nothing she knew had ever been so soft she thought as she fell asleep.

Abigail looked in on Ishtara from time to time.

"Shall we awaken her, my lady?"

"No, Laila, let her sleep until she is completely rested. There will be time enough after that to begin her training. She is a very special child and you will be her trainer and friend. You will guide her steps day by day and teach her the beginning lessons of the mysteries of Astarte."

Laila had long flowing reddish hair and fair skin. She was tall and regal in bearing. Her origins were Phoenician and from tribes farther north.

"I shall be honored and happy to be her friend and trainer, my lady."

Ishtara awakened and sat up. It was dark and she tried hard to remember where she was. Laila lit a lamp in the corner of the room and sat down beside her.

"Where am I?"

"You are safe. Do you remember coming here, the bath, and your name?"

"My name is Ho…Ishtara. My name is Ishtara now."

"Now and forever you are Ishtara. You will get used to it and become one with it in your own way."

"But what is my way? How does that happen?"

"It takes time. You will just know. It will become clear. There are no secrets here, just a process of awakening to everything that is within you."

"Did you go through this, too? Did your name change?"

"Yes, but we never talk about our first names. Do not ask me more. I am Laila forever. Come with me. The morning vespers are beginning and after that we will break our fast. You must be hungry."

"I am hungry. I do not think I have ever been this hungry!"

"You have had a long tiring experience. Come and take my hand."

Ishtara and Laila walked hand in hand into the gardens to a vesper spot where others were gathering. The music of harps and small golden bells played softly.

The girls began to sing in quiet harmony. Ishtara had never heard anything so lovely. There were only a few words to the song and soon Ishtara was singing with them. Abigail led them in chants praising Astarte and extolling her powers of love and prosperity for everyone.

Ishtara thought back to all the gossip and mean treatment she had received in the village where she grew up and how Ana and Tolah had taken her away. The only love she knew about was their love for her. Tears filled her eyes at the memories and she ached to see Ana and Tolah again. She suddenly missed them so much. Laila slipped her arm around Ishtara's waist and kissed her cheek.

The vespers ended and they walked in the gardens together.

"Tell me about your tears, Ishtara."

"We were singing about love and I began to miss Ana and Tolah, my parents. They were the only ones who loved me. Everyone else was mean and hateful. Is it bad to miss them, Laila?"

"No, of course it is not bad. They brought you here because they loved you and wanted to protect you. You must remember their love. It will give you strength, not weakness. Now you have moved on into a wonderful life that you agreed to.

"Do you remember agreeing to Abigail's questions when you came? It is all good! No need for tears, but smiles. Hold your head high and smile, Ishtara. Many blessings will continue to fill your heart."

"Yes, I remember."

Ishtara smiled a little as Laila gently dried her cheeks. She took her hand and led her into the banquet room to break their fast. All the girls were laughing and talking. They smiled at both of them and Ishtara's heart began to lift. The ache was soon gone and she was laughing, too.

Ana and Tolah found a quiet place on the outskirts of a small city in which to settle. They changed their names to Shuah and Noam. Only Malachi new where they lived in case Ishtara should ever need to know. But he knew she would never need to know. It would cause her downfall.

Ishtara was growing into a striking young woman. Her eyes were watchful and her demeanor quiet. Her smooth hair was raven black and her features were delicate. She had grown from a diminutive child to a woman of medium stature. Fortunately she did not yet look exactly like Majah, so she would not be easily recognized should someone be looking for Majah's daughter.

Ishtara's training was rigorous, not only in spiritual understanding of the powers and energies that she would wield, but physical training as well. She learned well the laws of spiritual warfare against evil and physical combat should she need to save herself from danger as she traveled to other temples and villages. The highest discipline was demanded of her by Laila, her teacher.

"Ishtara! A High Priestess must know how to use the power at all levels. It is wonderful to teach, meditate and heal, but you must be able to stay alive and safe to do those things. You must be aware of all that is around you and to find your way safely. You cannot be so heavenly that you forget the earthly dangers."

CHAPTER 8

Laila was Ishtara's first and dearest friend, and now her teacher and trainer as well. They lived together, studied together, and practiced all the arts together. All of their time was focused on discipline and work. Only when they took their meals with the others did they relax, laugh, and sing.

"You must focus your mind, Ishtara! When you rise into the realm of spiritual power, you must not let your mind go down to the lower vibrations! The physical world has many evils and will always be against you.

"You cannot trust that the outer world will lift you up or take care of you. You must stay in higher consciousness always. You must never let that lower realm take you over."

Ishtara spent many hours in her inner sanctuary in deep meditation following Laila's instructions. She began to slip the bonds of the material world and move easily into the higher realms. She could see the white light, color, and the sense the deep humming sound of the universe.

The feeling of floating was so heavenly that she wanted to let it carry her away forever. There was a strong tug of something pulling her back into her physical self. She tried to fight it until she heard Laila's voice.

"Ishtara, come back!"

It was Laila tugging on the hem of her tunic. She jumped and opened her eyes.

"What is the matter? Was I asleep?"

"No, you were not asleep. You changed the vibration of your physical body and disappeared. Do you know where you went?"

"I was floating over gardens somewhere, curious that the flowers had turned to stones. It was like a dream but it was dim and hazy and I guess a little frightening now that I think of it. My dreams are always very clear and colorful. They never turn dark like that."

They walked together out of the meditation room and into the gardens. The bright sunlight helped Ishtara recover her normal vibrational state.

"You must tell me what happened or what I have done wrong."

"You did nothing wrong. Changing your vibration is your next step in the training. This is useful to use when you are in danger or to go to a place that needs your help. You can move through crowds without attracting attention. You will need to control it and not just float away. You could have landed anywhere outside of the temple grounds and not known where you were or how to get back.

"For now you must not leave the temple until you are strong enough in the spiritual arts that you will not be influenced by the lower vibrations of the outside world. Now that you have changed your vibration and nearly floated away, we will start that lesson this afternoon."

"There is so much to learn! Every day there is something more and I always go to bed completely exhausted and spent."

"That is why you need to focus on the training until you do not feel drained, but energized. Moving into different states of consciousness will be effortless and you will effortlessly be in command of all aspects of yourself.

"You are exhausted now because everything is new and you are trying very hard, like climbing a mountain. Soon you will be at the top and it will seem natural and energizing. Being in command of the kingdom of your own being does that."

Daily Ishtara went through the exercises with Laila to anchor them in her subconscious mind. Laila was an excellent instructor and their lessons together were a joy to both. To her delight she was becoming stronger and more confident.

Each night she dreamed of her mother, Majah, smiling at her and reaching out to her, but she would awaken just before she could reach back and touch her. When she was fully awake she was somehow refreshed and strangely encouraged. She also remembered Ana's admonition never to reveal her dreams, so she told no one. They were her precious secret.

Malachi sent a message to the Temple of Astarte that a small city was under an attack of sickness. Ishtara immediately went to Laila and Abigail for permission to go there to help them. Abigail took Laila aside.

"Ana and Tolah, now Shuah and Noam, live in this small city. We must tell Ishtara before she can go there. It would be so dangerous for her to come upon them unexpectedly. Do you think she is strong and well-grounded enough that she can receive this?"

"We never know how strong we are until we are confronted with a test of that strength. We cannot refuse to let her go with us without upsetting her. We have always said that nothing is hidden. So now we must let her test herself."

This was the first time that Ishtara knew her foster parents names and where they lived. She was surprised.

"I never thought of meeting them again. I thought it would be forbidden once I became a priestess."

"We will go immediately, but you must remember that it is the name you must not respond to. If you respond to them they may call you by the name they gave you and that would be a disaster for you. Remember your promise to never respond to that name. It is very important! You would put yourself in great danger."

Ishtara could not remember what that name was and turned her thoughts away from trying to bring it to mind.

"I will keep my consciousness high and do what we are going there to do, which is to heal this illness. I promise I will not look for them. Most likely we would not even recognize each other."

Laila embraced her and took her hand.

"I will be by your side. This will be a big test for you but I am sure you are up to it."

The three of them went to the temple garden chapel, lay face down on soft thick mats, and opened themselves to receive and be obedient to guidance. They shared the vision, the image of the small city and the devastating illness.

They could see the caravan route and a caravan that was teeming with a spreading disease. The leader of the caravan sought to poison the people with the disease and take over the small city for its rich reputation in trading. The elders called upon the Temple of Astarte to assist them before everyone would die and all taken over by this evil.

Abigail went over the instructions with them.

"Ishtara and Laila, we must stay close together. We must not go anywhere alone. There are many people and the disease is strong. When the people show signs of recovering we will leave immediately and come back to the temple by the Secret Way that I have created for us."

"Ishtara, you must not become focused on finding Shuah and Noam. Those are the new names of your parents. We will be in disguise and show our faces to no one. Keep your focus on what we are there to do and know that the higher the consciousness we keep, the more quickly the disease will be defeated. We will travel there on foot to increase and stabilize our energy by anchoring it in the earth."

Ishtara was puzzled and a little confused.

"Would it not be faster to go there by the Secret Way, too?"

"It would be faster, but we might land in an unprotected place and frighten people by our sudden appearance. It is safe to return here because we will aim it at the temple gardens. I am glad that you asked, Ishtara. Do not hesitate to keep asking your questions so Laila and I can answer them for you."

CHAPTER 9

They dressed in peasant's garb, took a donkey from the stables, and started out after the darkness of night fell over the land. They avoided the well-traveled roads. The stars they used to guide them were bright. They kept to the shadows in the hills as much as possible, following sheep and goat paths.

Morning passed and the sun was high as they approached the city. A beggar hobbled toward them and held out a beggar's bowl. Ishtara recognized Malachi from Abigail's description and dropped a small pebble into the bowl. This was the agreed upon sign that would identify them to each other.

"Follow me," was the hoarse whisper. They followed him to a small hut behind the hills and waited for dark to again cover them.

The night was eerie in the small city, filled with moans and cries coming from everywhere as they walked into it. Abigail, Laila, and Ishtara worked quickly, going from house to house. The disease was foreign and powerful. It taxed their energy until they thought they would faint from exhaustion.

Malachi met them coming out of the last home they had to visit.

"The attack is defeated. The healing has begun. Go back to the temple now!"

Ishtara secretly hoped to see Shuah and Noam, but could not recognize anyone in the darkened rooms. Laila grabbed her arm and pulled her away toward the hills and the Secret Way.

"Hodesha?"

At the call, Ishtara turned back toward the last house and her hand slipped from Laila's. Laila stepped into the Secret Way just as Ishtara turned and they were parted. As Laila and Abigail were carried away in the wings of the higher energies they called to Ishtara, but Ishtara had allowed her consciousness to drop into the lower energies of that name and she could not hear them.

Something strange and powerful pulled Ishtara far away and she found herself spinning and falling, landing in a place in the desert. She stood up, dusted the sand from her robe, and shook it out of her sandals. She looked desperately around for Malachi, but he was nowhere to be seen. Then she remembered Abigail's admonition when she first came to the temple.

"You must never respond in any way to the name Hodesha, ever!"

She knew what she had done. She wandered for two days trying to find the Secret Way, but it was not there. She knew her consciousness was still stuck in the lower vibrations of "Hodesha the burning," and that was keeping her imprisoned.

As she stumbled along, a temple appeared on the horizon but it was not the golden Temple of Astarte. She kept walking toward it hoping to find help. A priest in a black robe and hood was on the steps, saw her, rushed out to get her and help her inside. He gave her water and led her to a bench where she nearly collapsed.

"I am Mishael – Servant of the High Priest of Baal."

Ishtara glanced up at him. He was beak nosed with a narrow face and cruel eyes. He looked strange to her. Foreign. Even a little frightening. Laila's words came back to her.

"You cannot find help in the outside world."

"What is this place? Where am I?"

"This is the Temple of Ba'al, my lady. And you are?"

"I am Ishtara of the Temple of Astarte. I somehow got lost on the way back to it."

"Well, you are safe here. Astarte is the consort of Ba'al, as you probably know."

Ishtara's mind was still fuzzy from the ordeal in the desert, but she remembered that now. He led her to a small cool room with a cot.

"Please, my lady, rest and I will bring you refreshments when you awaken."

"Thank you."

It seemed like only minutes when Ishtara awakened to strange sounds and chants. She sat up and looked around. It was dark and there was a small candle burning on a table in the corner and a shallow bowl of water and a towel. She got up, dipped her hands into the water and splashed her face and arms.

A fresh tunic was on the chair. She pulled off her dirty peasant's tunic and replaced it with the fresh one. Slowly she remembered all that had happened.

"They must have thought I was a peasant in these clothes."

She slowly walked out of the room into a hallway of the temple. A priest approached her smiling.

"We are happy to see you are awake and looking rested. Please, come with me. Hezion, the High Priest of Ba'al wishes to speak with you."

They walked down long ornate pillared halls and into a huge room with high vaulted ceilings that seemed to almost reach the sky. There were golden altars with black onyx sculptures of birds, fish, and all manner of frightening and unfamiliar animals. The place had none of the softness, beauty, colors, or fragrances of flowers of the Temple of Astarte. It was hard, cold and smelled slightly sour.

She was about to ask where the flowers were when the High Priest came forward with arms outstretched to greet her. He was tall, graceful, handsome of face, and had a wonderfully deep mellow voice that took her breath away.

"You are most welcome in the Temple of Ba'al, my lady! I understand that you have been through a harrowing experience in the desert. My priest found you approaching our temple. Do not be concerned or afraid. You are safe here. I am Hezion, High Priest of the great god, Ba'al. Come with me and we will break our fast together. You must be hungry."

Ishtara was still a little shaky from lack of food. She was sure she should not trust him, but his voice was reassuring, even comforting, and he was most engaging. She could not to trust anyone she did not know, but despite her training she was powerfully drawn to him. He seemed to have a strange magnetism that pulled at her mind and drove all spiritual thoughts from it.

They spent several days talking and walking through gardens of stone figures and dry sandy ponds. It was the garden she had dreamed about with flowers that were turned to stone. She could find no life in anything around her, only him.

"I will come to you tonight and we will be one with the passion of Astarte and Ba'al. That is our destiny. It is why you have at last come to me."

Ishtara fought that feeling with all her might and with everything she had been taught in order to free herself. Nothing seemed to work. Her mind was swirling downward into a dark abyss. She was fully in his power and could not find a way out. The will to fight it was ebbing and she was thoroughly frightened.

She walked as steadily as she could back to the room and closed the door. She collapsed on the bed, completely drained of energy, and fell asleep. Majah came to her in a dream.

"This is what happened to me, Ishtara. We made the love of Astarte and Ba'al, just as he said to you, and then I was abandoned by him. I was thrown out into the desert. I tried my powers to save myself, but I was still not fully recovered, lost and almost captured by the king's guard.

"They accused me of being a sorceress because I was alone in the desert. I turned my vibration and disappeared so they could not pursue me. So now run, Ishtara! It is a trap! Run away now before he can take you! Run out into the desert! Reclaim your power there and you will find the Secret Way. Get up and run now!"

Ishtara jumped up, pulled on her old tunic, grabbed her belongings, and ran out the door of the room. She could hear footsteps from far down the echoing hall and knew the High Priest was coming for her.

CHAPTER 10

"Focus, like Laila told me so many times. Focus my mind!"

Ishtara struggled to find that focus. It took all her energy and determination and she began to feel it slowly coming back to her. She ran as fast as she could down the halls and out of the front entrance of the temple. The walls around the temple grounds seemed far away, but she did not let fear take her concentration.

She ran hard and did not look back to see if someone were pursuing her. She felt like she could fly, running through the opening in the gate and into the cool desert night. Running until she had to stop, catch her breath, and then ran on.

She slowed to a walk when the temple was far out of sight behind her and the stars now lit her way. She sat down on a high hill and gazed at the stars, knowing they would guide her home if she could just remember which ones they were. Her consciousness was still a little fragmented.

"I must keep going. Somehow I will find the way back to the Temple of Astarte."

Ishtara came to a small oasis, dipped her hands into a small pool of water to drink and refresh herself. The she laid down under a palm plant and fell asleep. She dreamed that she was eating food and drinking wine. She woke up while it was still dark feeling surprisingly refreshed and the guiding stars she was looking for were very prominent and visible to her now.

She followed them for two days trusting their guidance feeding her body with light as she was taught to do. Presently she climbed over a hill and saw the small city where she had been hopefully not too long ago.

How much time had passed, how many days? The people were going about their usual business and there seemed to be no evidence of any sickness. She dared not approach it remembering what happened to her there. She turned away quickly and refocused her mind. Malachi in his beggar clothes was a short distance away motioning to her.

"Oh, Malachi! I am so glad to see you! I have been…"

"I know where you were, Ishtara, and I sent Majah to you in your dream because I knew you could not fight the powers of the High Priest alone. Since you are here, you must have recovered your focus and returned to the high state of mind. You have done well. Come. The Secret Way that Abigail and Laila are still holding in place is waiting for you."

Ishtara hugged Malachi and turned toward the Secret Way. She stepped forward and suddenly stood in the beautiful flower gardens of the Temple of Astarte. Laila ran to embrace her.

"Thank the graciousness of Astarte that you are home! That you are safe! Abigail said there was nothing I could do except keep the Secret Way in place. She said you must survive what happened on your own and you did!

"Come, the meal is being served. You look like you could use some nourishment."

She wanted to tell Laila that she wasn't alone, that Majah came to her in a dream and saved her, but she remembered Ana's admonition not to reveal her dreams. She kept the dream to herself.

Abigail instructed her never to acknowledge her former name in any way, even a small accidental way, and now she knew why.

Again Laila and Ishtara sat among the young women, eating delicious food, laughing and singing, and at peace. That night they slept in each other's arms and Ishtara dreamed of flowers, real flowers.

Ishtara knew that Samuel was the judge and prophet of Yahweh. His friendship with his god was amazing, enchanting, and inspiring. She had heard the story of his calling from this god as a child, and that the priest Eli guided him to dedicate himself to Yahweh. Samuel grew up faithfully serving his god and all Israel harkened to Samuel's words. She loved the story and admired his work with the people.

It was also a confusing time for Ishtara because Samuel banished all worship of Ba'al and Ashtaroth. The Asherah poles erected next to other altars represented the Mother Goddess of harvest and prosperity, and were precious to the Canaanites as well as the Phoenicians. Some of the Asherah poles were taken down and destroyed, but not all. Some that were taken down were mysteriously reconstructed and set back up.

It made her fear for her safety and the safety of the other priestesses. They all tended to stay close to the Temple of Astarte. The people of Israel were so fearful of the Philistines that they could only focus upon the danger of being attacked, so Asherah poles were ignored in many parts of the country.

The people had begun to demand that Samuel appoint a king to fight their battles for them and take care of them. Samuel warned the people that a king would not care about them except to tax them, take their best produce, herds and property.

A king would take their sons into war and their daughters into slavery, and their freedoms would be gone. But the people were afraid and continued to clamor for Samuel to appoint a king who would raise an army to protect them.

At the behest of God, Samuel anointed Saul, the son of Kish, a wealthy man of the tribe of Benjamin. The people loved Saul immediately. He was tall, handsome and blonde, like a god. When the people eagerly drew lots to elect him their king, he ran and hid among the camel baggage. The people chased after him, caught him, and placed a crown on his head. Ishtara wondered what manner of man could be a king, who ran and hid like a coward? It was all very strange to her.

Ishtara was about to be elevated to the office of High Priestess and turned her attention from Samuel to the final lessons she must learn and to memorize the rituals that would be performed. Laila, her faithful friend and trainer, was at her side.

"Laila, should it not be you who becomes the High Priestess? Why would I come before you?"

"No, dear one, I desire to remain a teacher and a trainer. This is my life's joy. I did not step into the path of the High Priestess because it is not my calling. But it is yours as it was your mother's."

It was a celebration that would continue for seven days. Every day the activities would highlight an aspect of the consciousness of a High Priestess. During this time Ishtara would be in seclusion to commune with Astarte. Her seclusion would culminate on the seventh morning with a ritual bath signifying cleansing away of the former way of being. Then she would step forward to put on the vestments of the High Priestess.

Abigail stayed nearby during Ishtara's time alone, bringing food and quietly attending to her needs. She assisted Ishtara putting on the robes, vestments, golden sandals, and golden symbols of Astarte. Then she was led by Abigail into the garden, through a Sacred Circle of dancing young priestesses, to the altar of flowers. Music from harps and golden bells filled the air as Abigail intoned the ritual blessing.

"The priestess becomes the High Priestess when she has the knowledge, experience, desire, and ability to dedicate herself to be of service to others and to the Divine Astarte. Ishtara, you have fulfilled these requirements and attained this high office. You have agreed to fulfill the duties of this high office. I declare now that you are a High Priestess of the Temple of Astarte. May you be forever blessed as you walk a new path in high consciousness and joy!"

Ishtara prayerfully took the golden chalice from Abigail, kissed it, lifted it in devotion to Astarte, and placed it on the altar among the flowers. Music from the harps and golden bells infused the air. Then dancing stopped at the signal from Abigail. The dancers knelt and sang a blessing, closing the service.

A lavish meal was served and, as always, there was laughter, giggling, and lively chatter among the girls. Ishtara and Laila eventually slipped away to their room to lie down and rest. Ishtara slept in Laila's arms replenishing her energy and an image of Majah moved through her dream issuing a blessing of her own.

CHAPTER 11

Ishtara's first task as High Priestess was to lift up in prayer and bless all the priestesses at the temple. She must meet with each one briefly, anoint her with a special oil of the flowers, commune soul to soul, bless and move to the next one. There were many so this took a few days. Then there was a closing ceremony and a banquet. While she completed this task, Abigail, Laila, and a few who were already anointed and blessed prepared to leave for a leper colony where their work was having a good effect.

"You will come to us, Ishtara, when you are complete here. We will send someone into the hills to bring you a clothing disguise and escort you safely to the colony. The Secret Way will not be used to arrive there because it would not have a clear focal point or target. It might open in the midst of the population and frighten the residents who do not understand such things."

Ishtara was happy to be free of her tasks for a short time so she could walk alone in the hills, bask in the sunshine and breathe with the breezes. She needed to take in all she had experienced in becoming a High Priestess. The place of meeting was not too far away. She carefully kept to areas where she would not be seen and watched for her escort.

An aging Samuel hiked through the low grassy hills to a favorite shady spot to rest and pray. He had ruled for many years and now his greatest and most unpleasant challenge was guiding an errant King Saul. His white hair and beard blew in the wind as he walked and tapped his walking stick on the stony ground. He often needed the renewal of silent communion with God.

He knew this was a place where wild animals roamed, although he was never approached by one until now. A young lioness was calling for her cub when she suddenly came upon Samuel. She growled a warning, bared her teeth, and circled him. He turned just as she lunged at him. Her claws raked his arm.

"Stop! Be still!" came a loud command from a female voice.

The lioness immediately backed off, turned and ran away.

Samuel had fallen down but was mostly unhurt. He slowly got up and looked at the beautiful woman standing a small distance away.

"Who are you? How do you command the lioness? Where do you come from? What god or gods do you worship?"

Ishtara smiled at him and approaching, touched the deep claw scratches on his arm. They disappeared immediately.

"I am Ishtara, a High Priestess of Astarte. I know your god. My god and your god are the same and we are given much power to do only what is good."

He looked at his healed arm and back at her.

"Only a god of good could send the lioness away in peace. Only a god of good could bless and heal. How do you come to be out here in the hills alone?"

"I am meeting someone who will shelter me with a disguise and escort me to the camp of the lepers. I hear the soldiers of King Saul have branded me a sorceress and seek my life. Anyone found with me would be killed along with me, so I should leave you quickly."

Samuel shook his head and reached out to her.

"I am Samuel. Please stay. We are safe here."

Ishtara looked around and back at him.

"King Saul does not know who you are. He does not know your name or what you look like. You will please come with me now, Ishtara. Again, I am Samuel, a judge and prophet of God, advisor to King Saul when he will listen to me, which is rare. I will take you where you will be safe until the one who is coming to escort you arrives."

She let him take her arm and went with him to his hermitage which was a cave hidden away in the cliffs.

"Even King Saul and his men cannot find me here. But his servants know all about me and about you as well, did you know that?"

"Yes. His servant, Malachi, is my protector. But I have been quite sheltered at the Temple of Astarte, so please tell me more of what you know, Samuel."

Samuel pushed some thick vines aside and they entered the cave. He lit a small oil lamp, pulled two benches out from the wall, and picked up an urn of water to pour for both of them.

Ishtara smiled as they sat down together. Surely this was a holy meeting with Samuel, the one she had seen in her dreams and admired since her childhood. It must be a divine appointment. She felt quiet and at peace in the cool of the cave.

Ishtara looked around at the simple hermitage of the holy man. It was such a contrast with the Temple of Astarte. His god must be a simple god, not requiring ornate altars and beautiful ceremonies. It was so peaceful and she wondered how it would be to live simply like this. She returned to the moment as Samuel offered her some figs.

"Have some of these to strengthen you."

She gratefully accepted, just realizing that she was hungry.

"As I mentioned Malachi has been my guardian and protector, always behind the scenes watching over me since I was born. He took me from the prison where my birth mother died to a safe home where I would be raised and cared for. I know that all of Saul's servants are known to Malachi and they revere him."

"Yes, I also know of him and of your birth mother, Majah."

"You knew my birth mother? How?"

"Saul was a simple and undisciplined man even after he became the king. He saw your beautiful mother and desired her. She refused him and he had her kidnapped and raped her. She became pregnant with you. He felt so guilty and was so afraid of what God would do to him, he decided to have her legally killed before you could be born by calling her a sorceress. I shamed him because he would not follow God's guidance.

"He did not know that he was too late. You were born before she died. Then he begged me to intercede with God for his sin now that the sorceress was dead, and reminded me that in condemning her, he acted according to God's law in Deuteronomy."

44

"Great Astarte! I am the daughter of King Saul? It is no wonder I have been in constant danger. I know I have done nothing to deserve being called a sorceress. The power you have seen me use is the power of your god and my god to do only good. It is God, not evil. I never publicly display that power for show as some evil ones do, but use it to heal and usually only within the temple confines."

Samuel smiled at her.

"Or when someone is attacked by a lioness? But you are right, we were alone, blessings be. I might have died right then, but God has one more task for me and sent you to me."

"Does Saul know about me? That I was rescued after being born, and that I live?"

"Yes. An envoy who carried out his order for your mother's death saw that your mother was pregnant and in labor. In his terror he promised Saul that the execution was carried out, but he knew if a child was born alive, the child or Saul could take revenge on him. He sent a warning to Saul just as he escaped to his own home, knowing Saul would occupy himself with finding and killing her, and forget about killing the envoy to keep his secret safe.

"Saul charged his spies to be thorough in seeking out sorceresses and put to death immediately any that were found, but to his consternation, they never could be sure that Majah's child was among them. No one knew what you looked like."

"Those poor women who did nothing wrong were killed because of me."

"Ishtara, it is not because of you, but because of Saul's disobedience to everything that is decent and the call of God. He will not obey God. God told him to kill all the Amalekites, but he let some of them get away and saved their king, Agog, because he liked his beautiful body.

"When he sins he comes running to me to fix things for him with God. He lives in waves of terror about everything and tortures himself constantly with that fear."

Ishtara sat quietly for a while to mull over what Samuel had said.

"I wish they could have been protected as I have been. I escape the dangers because Malachi's servants warn me during times when I must be away from the temple. They know who the spies are and remind me that I must trust no one. But I trust you, Samuel, because I know it is right."

Ishtara knew she was safe because she had seen Samuel in her dreams. She did not know who he was until now. She silently gave thanks for the childhood dreams in which she saw people she did not yet know, but knew she was destined to meet them one day. Still she did not reveal to him that it was because she saw him in her childhood dreams. She remembered never to reveal her dreams.

CHAPTER 12

They waited all day and night. The one who was to come for her did not arrive. A shepherd from the hills came just before dawn to tell Samuel that a man was found badly beaten by the road. Ishtara's heart froze. She looked desperately at Samuel.

"Great Astarte, were the guards following him? But why did they beat him? Surely they could have just followed him until he found me."

"On no, mistress, when he saw them he was leading them away from you and when the guards realized this, they beat him and left him for dead. But we found him and have bound his wounds. He will live. I must go."

He was gone, disappeared into the hills like a ghost. Samuel and Ishtara sat quietly throughout the morning, speaking softly and listening for anyone else who might be approaching. All was silent except for an occasional breeze moving the grasses. They passed the day in conversation, waiting for night.

"Where were you going when you left the temple, Ishtara?"

"I was going to meet Laila and other healers. We were working in a leper colony. The man I was to meet was bringing me a tattered robe as a disguise and some badly worn sandals. He would hide my robe and sandals and we would get them upon our return."

"Why did you not all go together?"

"I was finishing a high blessing ceremony with young priestesses in training. I was to catch up with them after I met this man and changed into the disguise. We try not to travel in a group which makes us conspicuous. There are those in the back country who wish to destroy Astarte and all who worship her."

Samuel stood and looked out of the doorway as the sun was setting. He turned to Ishtara.

"We must eat and then we will go to Rébekah, the widow who lives on the mountain. You can stay with her until the dangers are no longer close by. She will know when it is safe, but remember the dangers will always be everywhere as long as Saul lives."

Ishtara arranged some food onto a small table and they sat down to eat.

"My team will wonder what has happened to me. Laila will be searching the ethers for my vibration."

"The shepherd boy has already told her. He knows the leper colony. His mother is there. All is well."

Samuel reached for his walking staff that was leaning against the wall and at the same time handed a second one to Ishtara.

"Come, we will go to Rébekah."

They started up into the hills as night was falling and the stars were bright. The earth was so very quiet and peaceful. Through many twists and turns of the goat paths, they came upon a high cliff. Looking up at it, Ishtara wondered how they could climb up, especially in the dark. Then Samuel looked up gave a loud call.

"Samuel has come and brought a guest!"

Then they waited but Ishtara was not sure exactly what they were waiting for. After what seemed like a long time to her, there was a rustling and groaning overhead and soon a large basket appeared over their heads. Samuel took hold of the basket and guided it to the ground.

"Step in."

Ishtara gingerly stepped in holding onto the sides. The basket creaked under her feet. She was a little unsteady not sure what to expect.

"Sit down."

Samuel followed her in and the basket began to groan as it left the ground, being hoisted by someone pulling up the large vines that held it. The basket swung slightly as it rose up the side of the cliff. Ishtara clutched the side of the basket more tightly to steady herself. It continued its slow climb upward until it lurched suddenly to the side and two hands reached for her arms and pulled her out onto the ground. Two more arms pulled Samuel to safety at the top of the cliff.

Someone lit a torch. Samuel took Ishtara's arm and they followed the torch bearer through a wooded area into a clearing. A rather large hut loomed before them as the light from the torch played on the area. A woman appeared out of its darkened doorway.

"Samuel! Welcome! Who have you brought to me?"

"Rébekah! This is Ishtara, High Priestess of the Temple of Astarte. She has been in much danger from King Saul and his spies."

"Ishtara? Daughter of Majah! Welcome my child! Come inside. Let us light the lamps so I might see Majah's child at last!"

"You know me? You knew my mother?"

"Yes and loved her very much. Come and sit. We have much to discuss."

A serving girl brought a tray of wine, bread, and figs and placed it before them on a long table.

Ishtara turned to speak to Samuel but he was gone.

"Samuel?"

"He has returned to his place in the hills so he will not be missed. No one must suspect that he was with you. He will be safe in his hermit's cave and will continue on his way in the morning. You are safe here. That is what matters tonight."

"What is this place called, Rébekah?"

"This is Endor, my dear. Endor is a deeply mystical place. The energies here are different from anywhere else. They are an open door to the universe through which we travel to reach the seat of cosmic creation."

"What does this mean for the Temple of Astarte? Is the temple not also a place of greater cosmic expanse? Are we somehow limited at the temple and perhaps unable to spiritually advance its priestesses? Has it lost its divine purpose?"

"Oh no, Ishtara. The Temple is the garden where we plant the seeds of cosmic consciousness. We begin with the young women devoted to a higher way of being and train them in the arts of the powers and energies. Then they can come here to advance their skills and explore the cosmos, the eternal seat of creation."

"Is there a similar garden for young men on the same path?"

Ishtara thought of the Temple of Ba'al and its evil. Surely it could not be the dark Temple of Ba'al that trained priests.

49

"There was. It is the Temple of Ba'al. But the priests of Ba'al are stuck in temporal power and turn their energies to evil for their personal gain. They compete with each other to seduce women with their powers and promises of divine love."

"Yes, I have experienced that. Malachi sent my mother in a dream to warn me of the danger and I barely escaped."

Somehow it seemed all right to tell Rébekah about this dream. Rébekah smiled. It was as if she already knew.

"Yes, it was a difficult lesson and you now know that you must rise in consciousness to higher ways to avoid those snares. You will never again let your consciousness drop to a level where it can be captured and you would be destroyed.

"Now we have those cosmic lessons for you to learn and accomplish concerning that higher way. We will begin tomorrow. Tonight you must rest. No need to worry about Laila and Abigail. They know where you are and will eventually join us."

An exhausted Ishtara collapsed onto the soft bed in Rébekah's hut and went immediately to sleep. She slept late into the morning and awakened to the sound of Laila's voice calling her from her dreams. She was not sure if the experience with Samuel was a dream or resting in Majah's comforting arms was the dream.

"Awaken, Ishtara. You must have been very tired to sleep so long. Abigail and I are here to share in Rébekah's teachings with you."

Ishtara gasped and jumped up.

CHAPTER 13

"I am so sorry! I did not get to the leper colony to help you. Somehow I ended up here instead, but I am guessing you already know that."

Laila laughed and hugged her.

"Do not worry. We are accustomed to things not working out exactly as we planned and yet always for the best."

Ishtara hurried to splash water on her face and arms and pat them dry. They went into the living area to greet Abigail and Rébekah and sat down at the already laden table to break their fast. As they ate Rébekah began to speak.

"It seems, Ishtara, that you have excelled in your spiritual understanding and proficiency in the arts. You were not intended to go to the Temple of Ba'al until much later in your training, if ever since it has turned evil. And yet through an accident in letting your consciousness lower to the childhood ego state, you stumbled into it and survived. Also you easily stopped the lioness from continuing its attack on Samuel when you shouted the command at her, and that has brought you are here."

"How is it that am I rewarded for being in error? Should I not be admonished and some remedial lessons imposed?"

Rébekah moved closer to Ishtara and took her hand.

"Dear one, you have not failed nor done wrong, but excelled so quickly, far beyond the usual expectations. We would not send you back to earlier lessons that would stop your progress. We lead you forward on your path upward. You have already learned valuable lessons from your missteps.

"You will not lower your consciousness again because you have seen what caused you to do that and the result. And you will not give commands aloud as you did to the lioness and reveal yourself to those around you. You are just as powerful silently and perhaps more so. You can send a command through a focused thought and stay silent. Fortunately, it was Samuel alone who heard you and you are safe."

"Thank you, Rébekah. I have learned so much just in the last few minutes!"

Abigail smiled at Ishtara. "I was just remembering the little girl who was brought to us by Ana and Tolah. We did not know if Majah's child had survived, and there you stood! Suddenly I knew who you were and I was so happy. The prayers of every one of us that you had survived were answered."

"I have forgotten that name. But Shuah and Noam, I cannot forget them. Am I to know if they are well? Will I know when they pass on?"

"Ishtara, it needs to be enough that you remember them and their love for you. If that information comes to you, it is all right, but do not seek it out. You will draw yourself down if you do that. Do you understand?"

"Yes, I understand. I can see the difference now. I still shudder at remembering the feeling of the downward spiral and landing in a strange place in the desert trying to sort out what happened. Thank you for explaining it to me again."

Rébekah stood and announced what the next lesson would be.

"Tonight when daylight has completely faded, we will begin our exploration of the cosmos. We will travel together as one, bodiless and weightless, yet aware and able to ride on ancient energy paths. We will explore the ways of creation and draw all the thoughts about gods and goddesses together into the deep Truth of the One Creator of All. At the highest level of consciousness, there are no divisions, only Oneness."

After they broke their fast together late in the morning, and practiced some spiritual exercises that Rébekah taught them. They took naps in the afternoon and after dinner walked through the woods together to the Village of Endor. The villagers and elderly priestesses from the Temple of Astarte welcomed them joyfully. They sat together telling their stories and sharing spring watered wine and bread. Eventually they kissed each other's cheeks and said their goodbyes, eager for the sun to set and the new lesson to begin. They walked quickly back through the woods to Rébekah's. Just before dark they stepped into the Secret Way that Rébekah had prepared and appeared instantly in the Sacred Circle in the trees by the cliff.

The stars were brightening and the heavens turned into a blazing milky way. They seated themselves on the benches where they would leave their bodies as they lifted into the cosmic consciousness and traveled as one spirit.

It seemed only an instant had passed and they were back in the Sacred Circle in their bodies. But the sun was rising in the east. They looked at each other in surprise as Rébekah stood before them, smiling at their amazement.

"We must remember there is no time in the Creator. Time is a human construct by which we measure our earthly days and years. We did not sense its passage because time does not exist in spirit."

Ishtara was truly puzzled.

"How will we know what we have accomplished without the sense of time?"

Abigail and Laila just smiled. Rébekah moved closer to Ishtara and placed her hand on Ishtara's arm.

"My beloved one, the accomplishment is within you and as you continue your work, you will realize that you know so much more, sense so much more, and walk in a higher way. Earthly concerns will fade away and you will look upon and bless all you see. It cannot be explained in mere mortal terms. You will just know and the lioness will obey your love for her."

They instantly reappeared in Rébekah's hut and ate a light repast together to anchor their earthly energies. Ishtara and Laila took a long afternoon nap while Rébekah and Abigail enjoyed a quiet time together to remember their young years in the Temple of Astarte. Rébekah reveled in memories of her husband and greatest love, Adaiah, and their wonderful adventures together.

King Saul was tortured night and day by the thought that Majah's child had been born and was living somewhere in his kingdom. This child was surely a sorceress and casting spells to disturb him, punishing him for the death of her mother, and causing his terrors. He raged at those around him and even threw a spear at the innocent young harpist, David, who was engaged to play music to soothe him.

The spies of King Saul were sent out every day to find her. In their desperation to succeed so that Saul would not have them imprisoned or executed for their failure, a few women were accused of being this child of Majah, and were stoned to death. But still the nightmares and disturbances continued to plague Saul.

The spies eventually found the servant who nursed a baby for some foster parents. They threatened her until she told them all she could. They found Shuah and Noam in a small home outside of a city. They were aged and frail and when the spies began to torture them, the parents gave them the name of Hodesha, the burning. As Ana and Tolah, they never knew the name Ishtara, but knew that the name Hodesha was no longer hers. They were sure Hodesha could never be found because she did not exist.

Jarib was a young priest serving in the Temple of the Lord at Shiloh. He was tall, graceful, beautifully trimmed light brown beard and regal of bearing. His smile was warm and gentle, and the corners of his eyes crinkled when he laughed. He was well liked among the other priests and became a special favorite of Samuel.

Growing up he heard the stories of Samuel's miraculous birth and his calling to serve God. Jarib's deep desire was to go with Samuel and serve him, while he acted as a judge for the people of Israel. Samuel went from place to place giving divine judgment on moral and spiritual questions. Jarib was fascinated at Samuel's ability to touch the hearts of the people with his devotion to God.

He preferred not to be with Samuel when he went to visit King Saul. Saul was fierce and unpredictable, so instead he waited somewhere in the hills and prayed for Samuel's safe return.

Many times in their travels they passed at the foot of the high hill on which the Temple of Astarte sat. Jarib would look up at the shimmering golden marble edifice with awe, but with many questions in his mind.

"Why do you not go up to that temple and rebuke their worship of a goddess instead of Yahweh? Why do you allow them to continue in peace, their beliefs unchallenged?"

"Jarib, there are many corrections to be made, many judgments and answers to be given in our country, Israel. As you know I am busy night and day traveling, ruling, judging and praising God. Some of my work load is lessened by the good that others do. The young women there are doing a holy work for the good of all people. They do not disparage our belief in Yahweh, but work to support our belief along with theirs. In many places the Asherahs stand beside the altar of Yahweh with only love intended."

"Have you not had those very Asherahs torn down?"

"Yes, I did that until I learned better. Yahweh spoke to me that I should be at peace with all good people."

At that moment Ishtara and Laila came up the path toward the Temple. Ishtara stopped to acknowledge Samuel with a blessing. Jarib was struck by her beauty and grace. The sun shone on her raven black hair and Laila's reddish hair making them a striking pair. He wanted to say something to Ishtara, but words would not come and the moment passed. She and Laila continued on up toward the temple. He watched her as if in a trance until they were out of sight.

CHAPTER 14

"Samuel, she blessed you! Do you know her? She has taken my heart! I must meet her! Will you help me?"

"Jarib, I cannot call her out of the temple or arrange a meeting. The temple is a sacred place protected by Astarte, and only the priestesses may enter. I can pray about it and so must you. If it is right, it will come about in God's time and in God's way. We must move on now. People await our arrival in their villages. We must not disappoint them."

Samuel touched Jarib on the arm. Reluctantly, Jarib turned away from looking up at the temple and followed Samuel down into the next valley. He walked as if in a daze, hardly noticing the landscape around him. Hearing the tapping of Samuel's staff on the ground and glancing off of stones was the only thing that kept him from stumbling off the path himself.

Laila's eyes turned to watch Samuel and Jarib as they disappeared into the distance.

'Who was that man with Samuel, Ishtara? Do you know him?"

Shielding her eyes against the sun, Ishtara turned to look in their direction, too.

"No, Laila, I have not seen him before. Some of Samuel's priests travel with him as he goes about the business of judging, settling disputes, teaching and praying in the villages and cities."

"He could not take his eyes off you!"

"And you either!"

"No, I can see his mind. It is you, trust me."

"And why were you looking into his mind?"

"Because it is my job to know. Abigail will have more to teach you about that. But you are safe when I am with you."

Ishtara burst out laughing. She tugged on the front of her robe.

"We must be more aware and keep our robes and hoods close about us when we are away from the temple until we actually enter the gate and it is closed behind us. The only attention I want is from Astarte in blessing."

Laila could not help but tease a little.

"Are you sure, Ishtara? You look a little flushed in your cheeks."

"I am not flushed. It is warm in the sun. Let us go inside where it is cooler."

Laughing, they entered the gate and it swung closed behind them. They went to their sleeping room, shed their robes and sandals, and flopped down on the beds to rest a bit. It was nearly time for vespers and the evening meal.

"So, what did he look like? I mean when you saw his mind. What did his mind tell you about him?"

"He is mature and pure in his thoughts. If we see him again, I will tell you if his thoughts are still pure!"

"Now you are teasing me again."

"Yes and no. Being light hearted is not a sin but seeing someone else's mind is not to be toyed with. It is a sacred connection."

"Could he know you saw his mind?"

"Only if I wanted him to, and I did not. If I let him know, then I would be letting him into my mind and I rarely if ever would choose to do that."

"And when exactly might you choose to do that?"

"It is said that Astarte and Ba'al did that and became consorts in minds and hearts. I do not know that I care to have a consort. It is above my understanding and my station as a priestess. Astarte is gentle, loving and kind. Ba'al is, well, I do not know what."

"Cold and overpowering?"

"Yes, it seems so from what I have studied. Astarte and Ba'al are the light and dark sides of creation. It is as if the dark is always trying to overcome the light, but that is not how it is meant to be. Nothing can overcome light."

"From what I know of Yahweh from Samuel, He is both in One. One side tempers the other and they create a balance within the One.

That makes more sense to me. Not so frightening. The Temple of Ba'al is forbidding, many dark statues of strange animals everywhere and gardens with only rocks and stones. Even the High Priest was overpowering and evil in his intentions. I do not care to see that ever again!"

The music and bells sounded through their chambers, and they got up and walked to the vesper spot together. It was good to go through the prayers and songs to Astarte to quiet their minds. The evening meal was full of laughter and giggles, filling their minds with the joy of their lives at the temple and all its blessings.

Ishtara turned her attention again to Ba'al and the darkness that caused all the danger to the priestesses of the Temple of Astarte.

"Abigail, who are these beings? Are they just beliefs or fantasies?"

"Ba'al and Astarte are god and goddess, but not like humans walking the earth."

"How do they get such a hold on humanity that we build beautiful temples to them, tell stories of their powers, and as we are told, they demand worship? I love Astarte and love the life I have here, but how much truth is there in what we teach? How much is real and what is not?"

"I have asked these questions myself, Ishtara. I have even questioned belief in Yahweh, the One God over All."

They sat down in the temple garden of flowers together. A young priestess brought them cool drinks and refreshments.

"People have always believed in something above themselves. Something to make their lives better, give them good harvests, protection from enemies, and to vanquish whatever else causes them to be afraid. They could only ascribe human qualities to these beings, meaning that these beings must be praised for their favors, as humans need praise. The praise rises even higher into worship and rituals of worship."

"Does this mean that we are perpetuating falsehoods and lying to the people?"

"It means that we are supporting their unwavering belief in the good, their belief that they can do something to make their lives better, and that something more powerful than themselves will help them."

"What about when things do not go well and the harvests fail?"

"Their worship is more fervent. Their belief in the good becomes stronger and they have faith that it will all turn around again. And it does!

The seasons come and go naturally, but the people believe is it the gods and goddesses controlling everything and the change to the good is a reward for their devotion."

They sat quietly together contemplating the Truth of existence and how much that is taught and believed is not that Truth.

"We know that the Temple of Ba'al has gone dark and evil. How can that happen? It was supposed to be about abundance and good harvests, too."

"Sometimes the humans involved begin to believe that they themselves have the power and convince others they are somehow ordained from above. They love evil and spread fear in order to keep that power."

Ishtara thought for a while as they drank their cooled spring water and nibbled on the fresh baked cakes and sun warmed dates.

"I remember a story about the judge, Samson, who was involved with a Philistine woman. She betrayed him to the Philistine soldiers, they captured him, took him to Gaza, and he pulled down the temple of Dagon on his and everyone else's heads. Killed everyone including himself.

"Dagon was the god of fertility to the Philistines. How could they allow his statue to be pulled down and their temple destroyed? Was Sampson really that strong, or is that a myth, too? Somehow that myth meant something to the people of Israel. It is all so complicated!"

CHAPTER 15

"I know that Gaza is Philistine territory, enemies of Israel, but Abigail, I want to go there and learn more, and perhaps even about how the Temple of Ba'al could be allowed to turn evil. Ba'al is supposed to be the son of Dagon. I do not know how that works in the higher realms, whether he had a mother or did not need one. But I need to know more."

"What? Ishtara have you gone mad? Philistines would surely capture you and destroy you! They could do all manner of evil to you!"

"Yes, but if they thought I was a Phoenician sorceress, they might leave me alone! The Philistines and the Phoenicians are both sea peoples and not necessarily enemies."

"What can you possibly hope to gain from this?"

"I am not sure. I feel drawn, not the way I was overpowered in the Temple of Ba'al, but a beckoning to understand more."

"How will you go there? You cannot just walk all the way to Gaza. Of course you could, but it would be a very long and dangerous walk."

"I am thinking that I might book passage on a Phoenician ship bound for Gaza from Sidon. Then I could still travel as a High Priestess. The sorceress part would only come into play if I were threatened by Philistines."

"What do you believe draws you, Ishtara? Can you tell me?"

"Questions and the name that Majah gave me. The consort of Dagon was Ishara. How am I connected to Ishara? What did Majah know of Ishara that she gave me this name? What is their story? What kind of son was Ba'al? How did the priestesses at the Temple of Astarte know my name before I did?"

"These are worthy questions. Some I would like answered for myself. I will pray that you find the answers to them."

"One more thing, Abigail, do you know who Majah's parents were and how she came to the Temple of Astarte?"

"Only that there was a battle in which many were killed and whole villages were wiped out. A priest came to the temple carrying an infant, a baby girl, not more than a month old. We took her into the temple. The priest called her Majah. I do not know why. Perhaps he rescued her from dying parents and they told him that name. He left quickly and told us no more. She turned out to be an extraordinary spiritual being with understanding of the cosmic realms far beyond her years. We all loved her and I miss her."

Tears came to Abigail's eyes and Ishtara reached out and held her.

Laila came into the garden looking for Ishtara.

"There is someone at the gate asking for you, Ishtara."

"Who is it? Who would ask for me here at the temple? No one ever does that. Did he ask for me by my name?"

"He did not say a name but your description. I think we sort of know him. He is the priest who walks with Samuel on his travels to the towns and villages."

Ishtara was shocked and frightened. She kept repeating her question, does he know my name?

"This is Astarte's temple and only priestesses are allowed in. No one comes to our gate to ask for someone within the temple. Did he give his name?"

"He said his name is Jarib, Priest with Samuel the Prophet and Judge. He said he would be honored if you would receive him."

Ishtara relaxed a little and they broke out into giggles and laughter.

"I told you! I saw him looking at you when he was with Samuel!"

"Abigail, what should I do?"

"Well, Ishtara, will you receive your guest or not? It is up to you. It seems that you are always ready for adventure."

Ishtara slowly got up from the bench and started through the flowered paths toward the gate. She felt jittery and tried to calm herself with a few deep breaths. She turned to see if Laila was with her, but Laila was sitting with Abigail.

She approached the gate and saw him standing there smiling at her. There was no guile in his expression. His eyes were soft brown and trusting, almost innocent. She stopped and slowly pushed the gate open.

"I do not wish to intrude, priestess, but I would very much like to speak to you. May I come in?"

She turned to see Abigail and Laila still seated in the garden. That was reassuring.

"Yes. Just inside but no further. The temple does not receive visitors. Please come this way."

They walked to a far corner of the garden but staying in plain view of Abigail and Laila, and the gate.

"What is it that you want with me? Why are you here?"

"This may sound foolish, but my heart has been with you since the day I saw you walking to the temple. I do not know how else to say it. Is there a way we can sit and talk to share our thoughts? I very much want to be your friend if you can allow it."

Ishtara stood quietly with her eyes closed and praying silently.

"Great Astarte, guide me and show me how to respond to this man's love."

She opened her eyes and he was still smiling, patiently waiting.

"Come to me at Endor and Rébekah will guide us. Tomorrow in the early evening?"

"Yes, I know Endor. I will be there."

He walked to the gate, pushed it open, departed down the path and out of sight.

Ishtara finally stopped holding her breath. Her mind and body became a little quieter. Rébekah would know what to tell them.

Abigail and Laila were still sitting on the garden benches waiting for her. Laila jumped up and reached out her hand.

"Tell us! What did he want? Did you tell him your name?"

"No, I did not say my name. At first I feared he might be from King Saul. He wants to be my friend. That does not sound like a royal envoy. I am not sure how to go about this, but we will meet again at Endor tomorrow evening. Rébekah will know if I am safe and how to guide us."

Abigail rose from the bench and embraced Ishtara.

"Very wise. If his love is true, there is nothing to fear. You will know."

"I am not sure I will know anything! I have not been approached by a man except of course the evil priest of Ba'al. But that was hardly the same. I hope Rébekah can help me."

"I am sure she will, Ishtara. Be at peace until you now more. You will know if it is safe to tell him your name. We will be with you at Rébekah's for our next lesson on the cosmic realm. Then you can meet Jarib when he arrives."

The three walked into the temple where the evening meal was about to be served. Nothing more was said. They joined the joyful singing and laughter and most delicious food.

CHAPTER 16

Samuel sent a message to Ishtara to join him where they had seen the lioness.

"My body will no longer sustain my earthly life and is about to die. Please come to be with me in my last days. Come now. It will not be very long."

Ishtara created a Sacred Way and went immediately to Samuel's side. They walked to his hermitage cave where he laid down on his bed, clearly exhausted. Even the short distance left him breathless.

"I must tell you some things before I go."

Ishtara poured them both some water and sat down beside him.

"My sons did evil in the sight of the Lord and could not take my place. King Saul is a good warrior, but does not have the wit to rule according to the Laws of God. He is erratic and fearful.

"He believes that if you are alive, you are casting spells on him from somewhere in his kingdom and continually sends his spies to find you. Even if they found you, they would pass you by as if they had not. The spies have begun to banish the women from the kingdom and take them to where they will be safe, rather than wantonly pursuing and sometimes killing women accused of being sorcerers because of Saul's fearfulness."

"Samuel, you have been such a good friend. You are the father I never had. How will I go on without you?"

"I am old and ready to go. Even with your healing massages the pains no longer abate. You have seen me in your dreams and you will continue to see me. I will always be with you."

Ishtara knew what he meant. He had always been with her in dreams and always around her in spirit. They sat companionably together as the afternoon turned into evening.

A lioness appeared at the opening of the cave and looked at them for a long time. It was as if she remembered their encounter and was called to attend them in these last moments together. The lioness backed away a short distance and settled down in the grasses, seeming to just watch over them.

Samuel got up and they walked out into the evening and sat down in the grasses near the lioness. He laid down and slept peacefully with Ishtara at his side, awakening from time to time. They watched the setting sun and the stars becoming visible a few at a time. Then the whole sky was like a carpet of stars. Under that splendor of the heavens, Samuel's breathing ceased.

Ishtara gently placed his hands across this body and closed his eyes. She and the lioness watched over him for a time. Soon Ishtara had to leave and quietly sent the thought to the lioness to stay and guard him until someone came for him.

A shepherd sent word through to Malachi that Samuel had gone to sleep with the fathers. Jarib and his priests came to claim the body and carry it to their monastery near the tabernacle.

The lioness walked away into the bushes. All Israel gathered to mourn the passing of Samuel, for they loved him. Then they took his body home to Ramah, his own city, and buried him there.

King Saul was shocked and terrified at the news of Samuel's passing. What would he do without Samuel to intercede with God for him? His battle with the Philistines was coming soon and he had to have God on his side.

He ran to the tabernacle and fell on his face before the altar, clutching the Urim and Thummim in his hands. He cried out to God, but there was only the flapping of the tent roof for a response. Nothing more.

Completely rattled he went to his generals to review their battle plans again and again. Nothing would stay in his mind except loneliness and fear, the absence of Samuel, and the terrible silence of God.

"Noah, call the servants together right now! Is there a sorceress left in the kingdom? Someone must conjure up from the dead Samuel to advise me before the battles that will surely come! The Philistines are everywhere!"

"A sorceress, my lord? But they are all banished or dead at your orders!"

"There is always one hiding somewhere! You surely know that! One may even be my daughter born right here in the dungeon, born of Majah the sorceress. If she is alive, find her! All of you go out to search the villages and countryside. Come back when one is found!"

Noah bowed deeply, backed out of the room and turned to go.

"Hurry, you fool!"

Noah, the head servant, ran lamely down the halls into the servants' quarters calling for them. They came running to him wide eyed.

"What has happened, Noah? Is the king harmed? Is there an attack from the Philistines?"

He gathered them into the kitchen. They had a secret meeting place behind the huge hearth. They slipped into it so they could hear what Noah had to say without being overheard by Saul's guards.

"Worse! The king wants a sorceress to conjure the ghost of Samuel! We cannot disobey the king, but it would mean certain death to expose anyone who could conjure the dead or is even accused of it!"

They all began to whisper among themselves.

"What about the woman of Endor, Noah? She is wise. We will not tell the king about her. Let us go and find her first. If she can do this, she will make the decision herself. If she cannot, she will tell us what to do."

Noah nodded in agreement.

"You must not breathe a word of this. It would mean her death and perhaps ours as well. Not a word!"

The servants fearfully followed Noah to King Saul and listened to his raving about God and the battle coming soon. They stood very quietly with their heads down. Noah stepped forward and bowed deeply.

"Sire, we will go out to the villages and among the people to see if we can find a woman with a spirit, and we will report back to you."

"This must be kept secret, do you understand. No one else must know that the king is consulting a sorceress! If one of you tells anyone, I will have you all executed! Do you understand? All of you! And your families! Now go!"

The servants scurried away as quickly as possible back to the space behind the hearth and planned how each one would go in a different direction so they would not lead anyone to Endor.

Noah, went immediately to the hills behind the prison to find Malachi. He was the only one left who knew the way to Endor in the cliffs. Many of the older servants and guards who knew had already died.

Malachi was napping in his hut up the hill from the prison that he still lived in since before Majah was brought to the prison.

"Who goes there?"

Noah was panting from trotting up the hill with an urn of water on his shoulder.

"It is I, Noah, bringing your daily water and figs."

Malachi knew this was a signal. Whenever King Saul was on the rampage, someone brought him "daily water and figs."

"What is he roaring about now?"

Noah came in and sat the urn down beside a bench where he seated himself to catch his breath. Noah had once been strong but his hair was graying and his back was bent, revealing his aging physique and aching joints.

"Ever since Samuel passed away, he has been worse than ever. In the past he had thrown a spear at young David the harpist threatening to kill him. David fled to the hills with his friends where Jonathan hid them.

"Now David formed a small army and they went about the land fighting for whoever will hire them. It is said that the Philistines hired him to get King Saul's battle plans and he even offered to join them in battle against Saul's army. But the Philistines did not trust him and declined his offer."

Malachi sat up and took some of the water.

"Yes, yes, I know all of this. What is happening now?"

CHAPTER 17

"King Saul is terrified that the Philistines will defeat him and Israel now that Samuel is gone, and he has ordered us to find a sorceress to conjure the spirit of Samuel so he can ask him if God is with him in the battle against the Philistines. It is a terrible thing to ask of a woman, to admit she is a sorceress or even to be accused. She would surely be killed immediately if she agreed to do his bidding!"

Malachi reached for a fig and pondered this, again silently begging God to remove this crazy man from his charge.

"Leave me now, Noah, and come back tonight. I must think carefully about this. I am too old and lame to traipse back and forth to Endor, but someone must go and consult with Rébekah."

"The King has threatened to execute all of us and our families if word of this leaks out. The servants are all sworn to secrecy. They are so frightened as they go out pretending to look for a sorceress.

"It is strange that King Saul has demanded we find a sorceress when his soldiers have driven anyone accused out of the country. He even mentioned finding his daughter, Majah's child. I think he suspects we are all plotting something."

"No, I am sure he does not. I think he is just alone without Samuel and God, and his mind goes wild. Go now, and we will speak again tonight."

Noah bowed and left by a back way, returning to the Saul's fortress to see if any of the servants had come back. None had reported in. He avoided any chance meeting with the king and went down the back stairs to his quarters immediately. He prayed that Malachi would come up with something tonight. He lay down on his cot to pray and without meaning to, fell asleep.

A serving girl came to his quarters with food for his evening meal since he had not shown up at the servants' dinner table. Noah jerked awake and jumped up.

"How long have I slept? Is it night?"

"No, my lord, it is barely dusk. I thought you might be hungry so I brought your dinner to you since the table has already been cleared. Only a few elderly servants came to the meal. It seems that everyone else has gone somewhere."

Noah remembered sending the servants out to find a sorceress. They would not be back for a few days, pretending to search and too fearful to return.

"What is your name?"

"Hushim, my lord. Do you wish me to stay?"

It had been several years since his wife died and he was tempted to tell her to stay, but he had to get to Malachi now without any distractions or delays, or they would all die.

"No, Hushim. You may go. Only for now. I will send for you tonight when all is quiet."

She smiled shyly, nodded that she understood and it pleased her. Then she slowly backed out the door with the tray, clearly reluctant to leave.

Noah ate his food quickly and started out the door. A guard met him in the hallway.

"Noah, the king is summoning you right now!"

Hushim was returning for the meal leavings and almost ran into Noah.

"Hushim, go quietly and tell Malachi that I have been summoned by the king and will come to him as soon as I can. Tell no one else."

"I will, master. No one will see me."

She gathered up the remains of his dinner and went quickly to the kitchen. She knew there was a path behind the kitchen that led into the hills that Malachi once used and which was overgrown now. Covering herself with a dark brown robe, she pulled the hood over her head, and found her way through the tall grasses and fallen tree limbs on the path to find Malachi.

Ishtara, Abigail, Laila and Rébekah walked to the edge of the cliff where Ishtara and Samuel had been pulled up in a basket. They passed by and went to the Sacred Circle to the benches. For many years it had been Rébekah's secret place where she could contemplate the universe and the cosmic energies. It was also the place where she clearly sensed the presence of her love, Adaiah.

Ishtara felt chills as they walked into this Sacred Circle. It seemed to her that there was music of the spheres all around, yet not discernable to the ear. She sensed that Majah was standing near her. Rébekah touched her arm and smiled. I know what you are sensing and it is real. Please come and sit down with me."

The four sat down together and began to sing quietly to gather their energy and attune to each other until their vibration was as one. They sang the songs they had sung in the Temple of Astarte that carried the holy vibration. They felt themselves rising and expanding, becoming lighter and lighter. Soon it was as if they were looking down on the world from a high place.

Abigail sent the thought to them.

"We will now visit Majah's dimension, a cosmic dimension in which life is everlasting. No one is dead. Everyone transitions into the next experience in living where life continues to expand forever."

Abigail paused for a moment. She knew what Ishtara was thinking. Ishtara was eager to see her mother's dimension. Would she see her mother there and would her mother see her?

Rébekah turned to Ishtara and touched her arm.

"I understand your questions and your longing to see your mother, Majah. But the experience in the higher dimension is not like our physical experiences here on the earth. We are accustomed to embracing each other, kissing each other's cheeks, and breaking our fast together at a table with food. None of this exists in the higher dimension. But do not be disappointed. The connection is so much more fulfilling than the brief connection of an embrace. It is an eternal connection in spirit, a merging, almost impossible to describe in our words.

"We cannot dwell in this higher dimension now, but we will draw upon the spiritual truth that is there to create good in our lives and the lives of others. First we must trust that it is there and then we must rise in consciousness to make the connection with the Divine within us. The power is always here awaiting our recognition."

Immediately there was no passing of time, no effort on their part as they travelled through glorious light and celestial music. There was an inpouring of knowledge of the great mysteries, love and joy. It was as if they were reaching for the stars and the stars were beckoning to them.

Presently, Laila took Ishtara's hand and Ishtara felt herself coming back into earthly awareness. The trees were again surrounding them, the benches were beneath them and sweet breezes played through the grasses and leaves. She was ecstatic.

"That was so lovely! I want to stay there forever! But as Rébekah indicated, I did not see my mother as she would have been before I was born. And it is true, that the dimension is so fulfilling that all my longing was satisfied. I must believe that it will be forever and eternally so."

"This is the beginning cosmic lesson, Ishtara. We are always there even though it looks like we are always here. It is called by the Phoenicians, "Highest Heavens," our first home where the light never fails. We will allow the energies to reform into our normal state while we go to Rébekah's to rest. Laila and I will return to the Temple of Astarte and continue teaching the lessons to the young women who eagerly await us. You may wait here until you meet with Jarib."

Rébekah's expansive hut was always welcoming and relaxing, fresh sweet smelling grasses spread on the floor. A small meal was waiting for them and shortly after their refreshment, Abigail and Laila went back to the temple leaving Ishtara with Rébekah.

In the late evening Jarib came up the path from Endor where he was instructed by Rébekah to wait for her to send him a message. Ishtara was still deeply moved by their lesson and the powerful infilling of knowing she received.

She was surprised and a bit flustered to see Jarib approaching.

"Jarib? Rébekah?"

CHAPTER 18

"Do you remember that you invited me to meet you here? I waited in the Village of Endor for your lesson to conclude. Rébekah sent me a message when would be the perfect time to come here to meet you. I hope you are pleased to see me."

"But of course! Yes, I am happy that you are here as we planned."

They sat down on a bench and Rébekah brought them water, bread and olive oil with herbs in which to dip the bread. Jarib touched Ishtara's hand. His touch was warm and reassuring.

"Ishtara, I have been part of a search for the truth of how the Temple of Ba'al turned evil. It had been so important to our priesthood. I was about to go there for more training, not knowing it had become evil. Samuel stopped me from going and took me into his care and teaching. He sent me here because Rébekah and Adaiah had first-hand knowledge, having been there and experienced the energy of it. They were most fortunate to escape. I am only sorry that Adaiah was gone before I got here and I did not meet him.

"When I finally heard your name from Rébekah, Ishtara, I knew there was a connection with Dagon, the father of Ba'al in the realm of the gods. Dagon's consort is Ishara. Your mother, Majah, was a distant cousin of Delilah of the Philistines. When the Philistines killed Sampson, they murdered many. Majah was taken by her father to Sidon and then to the Temple of Astarte where she would be safe from the evils of Delilah and all the darkness she created. Unfortunately, there were such strong influences around Majah, that she was still in danger but less so at the temple. Her father never reappeared in her life."

Ishtara listened with rapt attention to every word. The pieces of her mother's life were falling into place and now she understood more about her own history.

"Did you know all of this before you saw Laila and me at the temple gate?"

"Yes, but I did not know it was you. I did not know your name. Samuel would not tell me. I am sure it was to keep me from making the connection and to keep you safe."

Rébekah came out of the hut and sat down with them.

"It is time for you both to look into your hearts and decide what your future will be. There has been a lot of information shared, and I am sure you, Ishtara, need a little time to take it all in. Would you like to spend some time in the Sacred Circle alone together?"

"No, Rébekah, I am much too excited, going to Majah's realm and now meeting Jarib here. I prefer to stay here and continue to talk with both of you until I can feel something is settled within me."

They talked on into the night until Ishtara felt confident enough to tell Jarib and Rébekah that she wanted to go to Gaza to learn about Dagon. She had told Abigail only a short time ago and Abigail was most disturbed by it.

"I have been planning how I might go to Gaza. I am sure the Phoenicians would be willing to receive me in Sidon and give me passage on a ship to Gaza. I do not think the Philistines will be interested in who I am, but I am sure I would be in no danger from them considering I have roots there."

Jarib was amazed and fascinated by Ishtara's desire to know more about Dagon and Ba'al.

"It is clear, Ishtara, that I must go with you. We have a joint purpose. We can learn so much more together. I will be easier if you are not alone to attract trouble from curious men."

"I had planned to be in disguise, Jarib, but I like your idea much better! I must go back to the temple now to inform Laila and Abigail, and to make other preparations. A High Priestess does not just walk away without insuring that the temple is in capable hands and safe. I know Abigail and Laila will help me do that."

They stayed the night in Rébekah's hut. The next morning Jarib and Ishtara bid each other a fond farewell, promising to return soon. Rébekah blessed them and reluctantly sent them on their way. She did not know what dangers they would face, where or from whom, but she would keep the high watch for them.

Abigail was happy to oversee the temple day to day events as she always had since Majah was taken and killed.

"A journey to Gaza? You have actually decided to go there!"

"I have to go, Abigail. Jarib will go with me. It might be just a matter of time before King Saul catches up with me and maybe targets the Temple of Astarte as well, declaring us all sorceresses."

Laila came from the temple and approached them.

"What is happening? Ishtara, have you decided?"

"Yes, Jarib and I will go to Gaza to learn about Dagon and Ishara, and get away from King Saul for a time. He will surely come to think that the Temple of Astarte harbors me and destroy us all."

"Then I am going with you, too. I must be with you and Jarib. I pray he will understand and welcome me."

"Of course he will welcome you, Laila! And I hope you know there will be dangers there as well as here."

"Yes, I do. But that will never keep me from your side."

Abigail performed a ritual protection blessing ending it with tears.

"Astarte keep you all safe! We will hold the High Watch here."

Ishtara, Laila, and Jarib sat down together at Rébekah's to plan the journey to Gaza that Ishtara desired to make. It was time to leave for their safety as well. The threats of King Saul to find and kill Ishtara were coming to them every day through Malachi's servants and shepherds who were pretending to search for her. Saul still did not know her name, but he was coming close to guessing that she might be a member of the Temple of Astarte.

Rébekah was as concerned as they all were.

"Saul can do nothing to me that Ba'al has not already done. But he must not find you, any of you. I have sent a message to young King Hiram in Sidon that you will be coming to him for protection. He is always eager to assist the Temple of Astarte, especially when there is trouble and danger. The temple and its priestesses are precious to him and to the wellbeing of all Phoenicians.

"Here is what you must do. Stay here until a small guarded caravan from King Hiram arrives in the valley below in a few days before dawn. When we are sure it is safe we will lower you down in the basket over the cliff so you can join it and you all will be safely carried to Sidon."

Ishtara looked at Jarib and Laila. The two of you do not have to go with me and be in danger, too. King Hiram's guards will take care of me."

Jarib and Laila were shocked. Laila took Ishtara's hand.

"Oh no, we will not leave you alone anywhere. We will go where you go."

Jarib smiled at them all and turned to Ishtara.

"Come with me to the Sacred Circle on the cliff. I must speak with you. There is much I need to tell you, alone."

"Go, children. Laila and I will prepare the evening meal."

Ishtara hesitatingly took Jarib's proffered arm and they walked through the woods to the Sacred Circle. They were quiet as they walked and Ishtara's uncertainty began to fade. She leaned a bit closer to him and felt the warmth of his arm in hers. It was comfortable and nice to be close to him. He smiled down at her and drew her arm a little tighter.

The special energy of the Sacred Circle enveloped them as they stepped into it. The trees were casting long shadows in the late afternoon and they chose a place to sit down where the sun was still shining though onto the benches.

Ishtara waited for Jarib to speak, uncertain of what she should do. Presently he took a deep breath and turned to her.

"I do not know how appropriate it is for a priest of Yahweh to speak to a priestess of Astarte, or how I should feel about you. But I must speak now or I may never get another chance. You are very near to my heart and I suppose it could be called love of a man for a woman. You are the most important person in the world to me and I want to be with you always."

Jarib stopped barely able to breathe and felt terror rising up through his whole being. His mind was screaming, "What if she says no? What if…"

Ishtara broke into his thoughts.

"I also do not know how to proceed, Jarib, but the answer is yes. I am sure we will find the way. Rébekah's guidance will come from her deep wisdom and bless us on our path of life."

Jarib's heart almost exploded with joy. He did not trust himself to speak, only to sit quietly holding her hand and watching the sun disappearing behind the trees. Slowly they got up from the bench and started back through the woods to share the meal Rébekah and Laila were finished preparing.

Rébekah and Laila had been surmising what was transpiring between Jarib and Ishtara. Laila had been teasing her about Jarib since they first saw him with Samuel.

CHAPTER 19

"My dear ones, I do know something about your situation, not too unlike mine with Adaiah, but a little different. I was a priestess of Astarte and he was a priest of Ba'al. There were no rules about loving each other, but the relationship between the temples of Ba'al and Astarte were more complicated. The High Priest tried to keep Adaiah from leaving by declaring there would be a marriage ceremony immediately. We did not consider marriage until we were forced into it. Then we realized that we had to flee immediately. There could have been punishments inflicted upon us decreed by the High Priest and that would have been torturous, especially for Adaiah. We escaped the instant the ceremony concluded.

"But yours is different. You are free. Your choices are up to you. Nothing can take away your priesthood that I know of, Jarib, and no one will take away your position as High Priestess at the Temple of Astarte. However, a decree could be sent out by someone in a position of power, such as a king, that you are no longer qualified to hold those positions by reason of your relationship or marriage. That might cast doubts among the people. But that is only my thought. The people who know you may not care about higher decrees and see you as the priests you have always been."

Laila and Ishtara glanced at each other. Their relationship had always been so close, closer than sisters. Would that change? Jarib stepped in almost as if he had read their minds.

"I have no wish to change anything between the two of you. I pray to be part of, but not instead of. Laila, I will not replace you in Ishtara's life and affections, and fervently pray that you will go with us wherever we are. Or let me go with the two of you, wherever you are. I am not sure which way to say it."

Ishtara and Laila burst out laughing. They both reached out and hugged Jarib.

"Come with us, Jarib, and let us be with you! No more talk of anyone being left out or separated."

Rébekah poured the wine in celebration. They drank enough to help them sleep. Tomorrow would begin a whole new exciting chapter in their lives.

It was nearly dawn when the message came to Rébekah that the small caravan was waiting in the valley. Letting three people down the cliff in the basket was a little frightening for those who had not done it before. Ishtara had done it with Samuel, but Laila and Jarib had not even suspected such a thing as their way off the cliffs. The creaking of the basket weaving and the swaying down the cliff unnerved Laila. It was a slow crawl for over six hundred feet down the side of the mountain cliff.

"I hope the Phoenician ships are better put together than this basket! Did you say that you and Samuel rode up the cliff to Rébekah's in this? It feels like it will come apart or the vines will break any minute!"

"We are quite safe. Rébekah's energy and blessing are with us. We are almost there."

They came to the ground with a thump and gingerly climbed out of the creaking basket. Ishtara led them down through the goat paths that she and Samuel had trod to the valley below. She guided them to Samuel's hermitage cave to await a signal from the caravan. Jarib stayed a little behind and sat on the upper branch of a small tree close by to watch.

It was a few hours before a messenger came from King Hiram's guard. Jarib spotted them and went to the cave to get Ishtara and Laila.

"We are here and ready for you. Please follow me."

Jarib was a little skeptical. He walked down from the cave and called out.

"How do we know this is actually King Hiram's guard and not someone from King Saul's guard?"

Ishtara stepped out of the cave, took Jarib's arm for support, and spoke to the messenger in Phoenician. The messenger answered in the correct Phoenician dialect.

"It is safe, Jarib. Saul's people would not speak Phoenician. They think it is an abomination to speak that language."

Laila came out, took Ishtara's hand, and they followed the messenger. The small caravan was by some trees. They were ushered into a closed wagon and handed disguises to put on. The wagons started off with a lurch nearly toppling them into each other. They managed to squirm into the hooded robes and rope sandals in the dark of the closed wagon. There were small benches along the sides to sit down on and wait as they bumped along the paths to a road that would take them to Sidon.

Jarib leaned out of the wagon and spoke to a guard.

"How far is Sidon? How long do we have to sit here in the dark?"

"Sidon is sixty miles. We are instructed to take you to the island of Tyre, which is much closer and a ship will be there for you to board. King Hiram's orders. When we are well out of King Saul's reach and into Samaria, you may safely come out of this wagon. Samaria is about half way. Jews do not go through Samaria. They believe it taints their purity."

That last comment brought a smirk from the other guards.

Jarib sank back into the wagon.

"Did you hear that?"

"Yes. Do the roads get any smoother?"

"They are caravan routes, and some places will be rutted and rough, but maybe better than these untraveled fields and hills."

Ishtara felt around in the wagon and found robes, pillows, and quilts piled under the benches and stacked in a corner. She pulled them out and passed them to Jarib and Laila.

"King Hiram has seen to our comfort as much as possible. Sending a royal entourage would have attracted attention. We can hope that the sea is calm when we get on a ship to Gaza!"

After several hours, Laila and Ishtara who were dozing were awakened by the sudden jolt of the wagon stopping. There were loud voices outside demanding to know who these wagons belonged to and where they were going. King Hiram's guard shouted back.

"These are King Hiram's wagons coming back to Sidon after delivering cedar wood to the Kings palaces. Can you not see the shields on the sides of the wagons? The wagons are empty."

Ishtara leaned toward Jarib.

"Do you think they are from King Saul?"

"No, I think they are a local militia guarding their territory."

The guards lifted a corner of the covering of their wagon, but Laila, Ishtara and Jarib hid under the coverings and hardly breathed until the flap was dropped down again.

It was a little while before the wagons lurched forward again.

"Do not worry," called King Hiram's guard. "We will not let them see you or take you. Our second wagon is full of weapons. We could not let them see those either. We would have killed them first. There were only a few men. More may have been hiding a distance away, waiting to see if they found something worth stealing. I am sure they will not return."

It seemed like forever until the guard announced that they were far enough into Samaria. They stopped the wagons at a well and the grateful three climbed out to stretch their legs. Jarib climbed out first, helped Ishtara and Laila down, and went to the well to draw water for them. They all went to separate locations close by to relieve themselves, and waited for the horses to be watered and the guards to be ready to move on.

"We must continue quickly. It is not good to stay in one place too long. That gives robbers and thieves time to attack."

Ishtara had not thought that robbers and thieves would be in this part of the country. She had heard that they would only be in the deserts to the south.

Thankfully the caravan routes got a little smoother as they headed north. They crossed the river into Galilee and started across a plain northwest toward the coast and Tyre.

"We will stop here at an inn and caravansary for the night. We are a little safer in Galilee. We will go toward the coast and Tyre in the morning."

They drove in through the gates and stopped in the middle of a huge courtyard. The guards helped them out of the wagon and took the wagons to a covered place in the main area of the caravansary.

The three looked around at the wall enclosing them with rooms on the upper floors and stables under them. Ishtara was a little concerned.

"This place is enclosed. What if King Saul's guard should come here? We would be trapped!"

The guard heard what she said.

"My lady, we are safer here than out on the road where we would meet those brigands again. Soldiers rarely come into these places because it frightens the caravan leaders and they might stop coming to this part of the country. That is not good for business."

CHAPTER 20

Jarib walked to the wagon to get the robes and pillows and returned with them. They climbed the stairs to the rooms above.

"I think King Saul will be looking for you much closer to him in Judea. These wagons have King Hiram's shield bolted onto the sides. I am sure the guards know when we are safe or they would not be King Hiram's special elite guard."

"Why would he send an elite guard for me? He does not even know me."

"Because Rébekah knows King Hiram and he is happy to help her when she asks. She told me this when I arrived at Endor and spoke about your travel plans."

"How did she know King Hiram?"

"She met him when she was a child, before she became a priestess. He wanted her betrothed to him, but her parents had already dedicated her to Astarte."

"Jarib, you seem to know more about me and my life than I do!"

"Priests are trusted with much knowledge and the people are willing and eager to tell the priests all about their lives and everything they know. It is a way of making them feel closer to Yahweh."

"And does it make them closer to Yahweh?"

"If in their hearts they feel closer to Yahweh, then yes."

The rooms had filled up early by caravan people. Laila and Ishtara found a large corner room that was still empty and set about arranging the robes and pillows so they could all rest comfortably. Presently, the guards brought food and wine for their dinner and bid them good night.

The gate of the caravansary creaked and rattled open at dawn and a large ornate carriage came in, horses prancing and dripping with sweat. Laila jumped up first and went to the door. Ishtara came to the door behind her and peered out.

"It is a carriage from King Hiram!"

Jarib stepped out onto the balcony and trotted down the stairs.

"Either this is bad news or the carriage is for us to go to Tyre in style."

He walked to the carriage and addressed the guard.

"Sir, who is this carriage for?"

"Who might you be?"

"I am Jarib, a priest of Eli and Samuel."

"Are you with the High Priestess, Ishtara?"

"Yes, that is true. Are you here for us?"

The guard hopped down from his horse and opened the carriage doors.

"You all must be ready to go as soon as we water and cool down the horses."

Jarib went back up the stairs to the room, gathered the robes and pillows and took them down to the wagon. Ishtara and Laila followed him and a guard helped them into the carriage. Jarib entered the carriage when the horses were brought back and harnessed again. Immediately the guards turned the carriage back toward the gate and urged the horses into a gallop.

Laila clung to a hand hold on the side of the interior.

"This is almost worse that the swinging of the basket at Rébekah's!"

The carriage swung onto a caravan route and continued the gallop.

"Jarib, why are we going so fast? Are we being pursued?"

"It is just few more miles to the border of Phoenicia and then I think they will slow down. They never like to linger outside of their territory."

As Jarib had surmised, the carriage slowed and the horses continued at a walk. A guard rode up beside the carriage window.

"We are in Phoenicia, Ladies, and soon coming to Tyre."

Ishtara sank back into the plush seat and heaved a sigh.

"Bless great Astarte, this part is nearly over!"

The city of Tyre was built on the shore of the Great Sea and extended onto an island in the harbor. There were small boats near the shore and ships anchored as far as the eye could see. The bustling activity on the docks spilled over into the city streets. Goods were being loaded and unloaded, filling markets along the coast and inland.

Ishtara and Laila stood on a wall looking out over Tyre and the bay, astonished at the expanse of commerce and buildings along the shore. Caravans were parked everywhere along the eastern edge of the city. The smells of dead fish, strange cargoes, and animal smells that wafted up on the breezes were overpowering and made them feel ill.

Jarib helped them down from the wall and guided them across the sandy roadside to an inn.

"Come. We are exhausted and we must rest. King Hiram's servants are here to take care of us for a few days or until our ship is ready."

They crossed the road with Jarib and entered the wide doorway. The inn was spacious with many rooms, a large decorated dining room, and tiled baths. Specially appointed servants hurried to meet them and take them to a quiet, beautiful room filled with comfortable cushions and lovely drapes where they could rest and eat. They laid down on great recliners beside a board spread with fresh fruit, fish, meats, bread and figs. Vases of flowers were in the corners of the room and a few on the board. They were a pleasant relief from the smells of the harbor.

Ishtara was sure she couldn't eat. She leaned against Jarib's shoulder and immediately dozed off. Laila was sleepily reaching for some fruit and pulled more pillows closer to support her. They were awakened by the sound of bells. Ishtara thought she was still at the temple, but realized they were not the small silver bells of the temple. They were camel bells of all sizes and bells to ring for servants.

Servants came to escort them to their rooms on the upper floor. There was a private bath in each one and fresh robes, tunics, and sandals laid out for them. A servant stood ready in each room to assist them with their bath and dressing.

They walked out of their rooms and joined each other on a balcony that ran the length of the building. It was late evening and the shoreline was ablaze with torches. The crews were still working on the docks. Their shouts could be heard far into the night.

The three walked downstairs to a large beautifully decorated dining room and were immediately greeted and seated by their servants.

"And I thought I could make this trip alone! I am so grateful for the two of you coming with me. Everything is so different and more difficult that I thought it would be. I would have been lost!"

They all laughed. A servant came to recommend some selections, bowed and took their dinner order to the kitchens.

Laila look worried and they looked at her quizzically.

"I do not think I want to sleep in a room alone. It does not feel safe. There is too much strangeness around us. Could we all sleep in the same room again?"

"Of course we can. I will move our few belongings into Ishtara's room and we will all stay there."

Ishtara nodded and Laila heaved a sigh of relief. The dinner was served and they were ready to eat, be done with the day, and go to the room for the night. A cool breeze from the Great Sea cooled the room a little and all three were asleep almost immediately.

CHAPTER 21

The clatter and roar of the city rose to a crescendo just before dawn when the activity on the docks and in the city lurched into gear. The loading and unloading of the ships picked up intensity and the shouts of the sailors and merchants signaled the beginning of another busy day.

It was still dark when Jarib, Ishtara and Laila got up. Jarib and Laila went to their respective rooms to take their baths and dress in the tunics and sandals left for them by the servants. Laila wondered if the servants were surprised that she was not in her room when they brought the clothes and bath fragrances, oils and towels. But then they would know when they brought Ishtara's supplies to her room and saw all three of them sleeping there.

After they bathed and dressed they went down to the dining room to break their fast. Their special servants came rushing to greet them, bringing delicacies of fruit, kefirs, breads, cucumbers, and sliced meats. Finger bowls of lemon water and small towels were placed on the table as well.

"This is amazing. As a priest I have been accustomed to eating figs, grains, and berries growing along the paths that Samuel and I took on our travels. People in the villages offered us bread and fish, but that might be only once a day."

"As long as you are in Phoenicia with the High Priestess of Astarte, you will be fed three times a day and more!"

They all three laughed.

Two of King Hiram's envoys came into the dining room and to their table.

"Your ship will be sailing to Gaza in the late morning today when the tide is going out. Please by ready and we will come back shortly and escort you to the ship."

They turned and left as abruptly as they came in. Special servants came to the table to tell them that bundles for packing were placed in their rooms.

"We will pack your things and there will be heavy robes for you to wear because it will be cold and windy on the sea."

Ishara, Jarib, and Laila looked at each other in astonishment. Jarib got up from the table.

"Now we shall begin! I have not been on a ship before and I am sure you two have not been on one either. Hopefully there will be a room where we can shelter from the wind. I pray that Yahweh and the captain will look out for us!"

Ishtara and Laila took a moment to say a prayer to Astarte to protect and guide them.

The guard came with a small carriage to make them to the dock. They went past the souks and along the shore. Laila was delighted.

"Everything comes from places so far away! I would love to stop and look at everything, but I am sure we do not have time. Perhaps on our way back."

Ishtara was focused on the harbor and its activity. Everyone was in a hurry. Captains were yelling at the sailors to either pack the sails or put them up, she couldn't tell which. Along with the noise, once again they were overwhelmed by the smells that seemed to burst upon them. They covered their noses with the sleeve of their robes.

"Jarib, there are so many ships! How do they know which one is ours?"

The carriage came to a stop half way down the dock. The guard unloaded the bundles while Ishtara, Laila, and Jarib stepped down from the carriage. The other guard motioned them to follow and they wove their way through crates, bundles, fishing nets and other equipment. At the end of the dock was a small boat.

"This boat will take you to the ship that is anchored farther out. The name of the ship is 'The Barekbaal' which means Ba'al has blessed."

Ishtara looked doubtfully at the boat which was pitching in the waves. They had to climb down a ladder and step into it. Jarib took her arm and guided her down the rungs. The oarsman reached for her hand as he kept the boat steady and close as possible to the ladder. Laila came next, certain she would fall into the water and be drowned. Jarib came last, stepped into the boat, and they were on their way.

The oarsman wove the boat through a myriad of barges, boats of all sizes, dodging anchors and debris. They went farther and farther from the dock until at last they could see the name on the side of a ship. It was not the largest ship of all the ones they could see. The oarsman assured them that it was lighter and faster than the others, just right for a trip to Gaza.

"Jarib, how will we get aboard? That would be a very long ladder."

"You will be brought up over the side to the lower level and climb an inside ladder to the deck."

The oarsman's answer did little to clarify how that would happen or to quiet Ishtara and Laila's nerves. As they approached the ship, a sailor called out and directed the oarsman to the cargo opening and a platform being lowered. The wind was picking up making everything seem so unsteady. The oarsman maneuvered the boat to the side of the ship and pulled it close to almost touching. The waves slapped at the sides rocking both boat and ship. Jarib reached out to a rope coming down from the platform to help steady the boat.

Ishtara and Laila moved toward the platform with the help of Jarib and the oarsman. They climbed onto the platform on hands and knees. Jarib was right behind them holding onto them while the platform was drawn up slightly and into the side of the ship. A hatch banged shut and they were inside. A sailor met them and guided them up to the deck.

The captain of the ship met them and apologized profusely for the way they had to board.

"King Hiram needed us to leave today instead of tomorrow, so we had to move quickly and there was no way we could have the way cleared to the dock for you to board in the normal way.

"We could not move this ship through the crowded harbor to the dock on short notice or we would lose the tide and our sail away schedule. I am sure King Hiram will not be pleased when he hears of it, but you are here and safe. Please come up to my cabin where you will be out of the wind and be warm and comfortable. There is food and wine, and benches with large pillows and quilts."

They climbed the ornate steps to the captain's level. The captain's cabin was a surprise. It was plush with beautiful furniture and colorful draperies. Images of Ba'al and Astarte were on the walls and the windows had shutters that could be opened so they could see the rest of the ship, the sky and the sea.

They could hear the roar of the sails being hoisted, the oars grinding on the oarlocks as they dipped into the water, and feel the ship pushing out of the bay onto the Great Sea. It gently rocked with the waves and listed slightly when it was turned into the right and left, getting to the shipping channel to head south.

CHAPTER 22

Jarib spent most of the trip on deck watching the sailors and learning something of their craft. The weather was fair so the sailing was smooth and there was a good north to south wind carrying them quickly along.

Laila's stomach was upset through the whole trip. She spent most of the time lying flat on a bench and sipping a potion of bitters for sea sickness that the captain gave her. Ishtara split her time between caring for Laila and standing on deck with Jarib. It was exhilarating to feel the wind in her face and hair as the ship almost flew over the waves.

"What are you planning to do when we get to Gaza, Ishtara? Where will we go when we get off this ship?"

"King Hiram's people have said to go to an inn located next to the Temple of Dagon. Our lodging is paid for and the owner is Hannibal, a Phoenician. From there I want to find more information about Dagon and Ishara. Perhaps there is a library or something. There will surely be priests and priestesses who can tell me more. If there is a connection with my mother, I want to find it. I want to know where she got my name and what it meant to her and for me."

"We must remember that in Gaza we will be in the land of the Philistines, not the Phoenicians, Ishtara. I wonder how a Phoenician can own an inn there."

"It could be that King Hiram's people stay there when they come in and out of Gaza. Just a guess. We will know when we get to it."

A sailor pointed out the fish swimming around the ship. They were all colors of the rainbow, some very large, some jumping and flying. Ishtara and Jarib were fascinated and watched them for an hour. Ishtara wanted

Laila to see them, but she was a bit green like some of the fish and could not stand up or leave the captain's cabin.

Late in the evening they turned into the port at Gaza. There was a berth for the ship beside the main dock and Ishtara was most grateful. She did not relish the thought of being lowered over the side of the ship onto a small boat again.

The captain and a sailor helped Laila out of the cabin, down the steps, off the ship and onto the dock. She was so relieved to be on land again that did not rock or sway. The potion was helping and her nausea soon subsided.

"Laila! I am so sorry you were ill. I feel so guilty bringing you along on this trip."

"Oh, no! Ishtara. I insisted on coming and I would again. Maybe the next time I will not be so sick. At least that is what the captain said."

The Temple of Dagon was not easy to miss. It was huge with massive pillars on either side of a statue of Dagon that reached up to the roof of the temple. Ishtara had to crane her neck to see to the top of it.

They walked around the temple's open court yard until they came to the inn. It was spacious and quite impressive. The owner, Hannibal, greeted them graciously and showed them to their rooms. Their bundles were already in the rooms.

Laila was still a bit unsteady, so they decided to rest and eat dinner later on. Hannibal brought them wine and a powder to put in Laila's wine to quiet and steady her.

"Hannibal, where do you think I can begin to learn more about Dagon and Ishara?"

"Do you wish to worship Dagon, my lady?"

"No, I worship Astarte. I am her High Priestess. My mother died when I was born. She gave me the name, Ishtara. Did she have a connection with Ishara? Ba'al is the son of Dagon and Ishara. What caused the Temple of Ba'al to turn to evil? I want to know more about my heritage and what the realm of gods and goddesses means to my life."

"I see. Perhaps I can bring someone here to the inn to speak with you and guide you in your search. Even though we are at peace with the Philistines, there are those who could be dangerous to you. They are at war with King Saul and may not understand who you are as High Priestess of Astarte.

"David, Saul's former musician and friend of Saul's son Jonathan, and his six hundred men are at Ziklag, in Philistine territory. Saul has been seeking his life and he has hidden himself in Philistine territory. Achish, son of the king of Gath, gave him Ziklag for his home and David has lived in Philistine territory ever since in return for giving them information about Saul's battle plans. If he deceives Achish and goes back to Israel, it will be very bad for anyone who has formerly lived in Israel."

She thanked Hannibal for his kind assistance and concern for her safety. Ishtara agreed to meet a person that Hannibal would bring on the morrow. She and Jarib spent the evening trying to take in all that he said about the situation with the Philistines. She knew the stories about King Saul and David, but not that he was here in Philistia.

Their dinner was served late when Laila was feeling much better and her appetite had returned. They spent the dinner time discussing the plan that Ishtara wanted to implement. Jarib added what he knew about the activities of David and his men and how deceptive he was.

"The situation in Philistia could become very volatile if he attacks or comes here. We need to be sure we are not identified with him or King Saul. The Philistines could think we are spies."

"You are scaring me, Jarib. I am so sorry to bring you both into this. We will stay close to the Temple of Dagon and its priesthood, and not draw attention to ourselves. Hannibal will book passage for us on a Phoenician ship if we need to leave quickly."

The next morning Hannibal brought a priest to meet Ishtara. "High Priestess Ishtara, this is the High Priest Melqart."

"An honor. How may I serve you, High Priestess?"

"I am honored that you have come to meet me, Melqart. I am here to learn about Dagon and Ishara and what connection this might have to my mother, Majah, who gave me the name Ishtara. I have no understanding of who she was or what influenced her to give me that name at my birth and her immediate death."

"Ishara was a goddess of many things depending upon the culture in which she was worshipped. She came to be seen as a 'goddess of medicine' whose pity was invoked in case of illness. She was a love goddess, goddess of binding promise, a goddess of the oath. She was associated with the underworld. She is called the mother of the Sebitti, the Seven Stars. The Sebitti are a group of seven minor war gods. They are the children of the god Anu and are of good and evil influence.

"Anu is the divine personification of the sky, supreme god, and ancestor of all the deities. Anu was believed to be the supreme source of all authority, for the other gods and for all mortal rulers, and he is the one who contains the entire universe."

CHAPTER 23

Ishtara was amazed and engrossed in trying to understand what this might have to do with her mother and herself but Melqart seemed to read her thoughts.

"If you wish to find something of your mother in what I have told you, look for those things at the human level that embody love and goodness. Her ancestry can only be learned at the human level. The level of the gods will not give you that information."

"What of Dagon? Is he the father of Ba'al as I have heard?"

"The name Dagon means fish or grain, depending upon who is speaking of him. He is a god of fertility. His wife was called Belatu, which means lady, and she is the sister of Astarte. Some say he is the father of Ba'al and some say Anu is his father. Godly connections are not like human families. They are all subject to interpretation according to the peoples who worship them."

Ishtara glanced at Jarib and Laila.

"Perhaps I have come on a fool's errand."

"Oh no, my lady! The pursuit of knowledge and understanding is never a fool's errand. It is your question that has led you here and perhaps the answer is not as you imagined or hoped it might be. But it is still an answer and will live within you until it is clarified in the right way that will add to your understanding."

"High Priest Melqart, you have been so very kind and I am thankful for all you have told me. I will continue to think on these things as I continue my quest."

"Come to the temple of Dagon this afternoon, all of you, and I will conduct you through it and explain our symbolism in the paintings on the walls and ceilings, and some of our history."

That afternoon, Ishtara, Laila, and Jarib went to the temple's outer court and met High Priest Melqart. Their tour was fascinating and the vastness of the temple still took their breath away. The symbols were beautifully painted on walls and ceilings, but Ishtara wondered at the statues and carvings of Dagon as half man and half fish. It was all very strange but she began to have a vision of the upper world as fluid and containing everything that could bless or beset humans.

"Perhaps it is as Abigail said, that we create the gods and goddesses after our own images to fill our needs and quiet our fears. Every culture has its own fears and needs that are a little different from the others, so the gods and goddesses are different as well."

Jarib was beside her and heard what she said.

"You and Abigail have discussed these things?"

"Yes. I have always wondered if religions were made up to ward off fears and fulfill hopes and dreams. Where else could they come from and for what other purpose?"

They sat down on a bench by a fountain and Melqart quietly left them to rest.

Presently Ishtara began to look around for Laila. She called out to her but there was no answer. Jarib became alarmed and they both jumped up and began to search for her.

"Where could she be and where has Melqart gone?"

"Would she go back to the inn if she did not feel well?"

"Surely not without telling us!"

They ran back to the inn. Mohammed saw them rush in the door.

"What has happened?"

Ishtara was nearly hysterical.

"It is Laila! She was with us and then she was gone! We thought she might have come here."

"She has not come here. No one has come here yet today. Might she have gone to the markets?"

95

They hurried back to the temple looking for Melqart. He came down the steps of the outer court and rushed over to them. Jarib stepped from behind Ishtara.

"Laila has disappeared, Melqart! Do you know where she is?"

"I do not know, but I do know that David and his brigands have attacked two Amalekite villages and burned them to the ground. His Village of Ziklag was destroyed by the Amalekites and his wives and servants taken."

"Why would someone take Laila? For what?"

"I think word has gotten around that you all are here from Phoenicia, and from the Temple of Astarte. They believe you are somehow connected with King Saul and his enemy David. Now David is everyone's enemy. People are going crazy and looking for ways of revenge."

Ishtara was nearly in tears and Jarib held her tight.

"What can we do?"

"I will ask people around the temple if they have seen her. I am sure Hannibal may be of help. He has the ear of the Phoenician military and they may be able to find her."

Hannibal sprang into action, sending messages to the docks and the military attaché there. They sent messages to their ground troops in the area and mobilized them in the direction of the Amalekite villages, scouring the area, farm, villages, and strongholds. Some even went to find David and his men.

"If they took David's people, they might also have Laila and he would be going after all of them."

"We cannot just sit here and wait!"

Jarib went to the docks to find the Phoenician attachés office.

"We need to go with your officers to find Laila. You do not know her or what she looks like."

Hesitantly, he sent a message to one of the officers who agreed to take them. The officer arrived with horses for them. Ishtara was not daunted. She climbed aboard with a little help, and Jarib rode the other one. Robes flying behind them they galloped down the road toward the area of Ziklag and the other destroyed villages.

They soon caught up with the rear guard of the military.

"Who is going to find David and his men?"

A soldier pointed to a group of soldiers that were breaking away from the main body. Jarib, Ishtara, and the officer turned and rode after them. They soon picked up the tracks left by David's men and questioned anyone they saw along the way. The local people just pointed in a direction and they kept riding.

Eventually there was a rather large young man standing beside his horse on the road before them and they stopped.

"Who are you and why do you pursue me? Are you from King Saul?"

"We are Phoenicians looking for a priestess who was taken from the Temple of Dagon. Who are you?"

"I am called David."

He motioned for his men to come out of hiding. Ishtara was taken aback at the sight of six hundred shaggy dirty men coming out of the scrub on the hills leading their horses. Jarib rode close beside her.

The officer rode forward and dismounted and asked if they might ride along in search for the prisoners, those that were taken.

"You may come with us and help us destroy these Amalekite enemies once and for all!"

"We only seek a priestess who was taken from the Temple of Dagon. She is a visitor from Tyre and the Temple of Astarte. We do not wish to bring the whole Phoenician army of King Hiram into this. We will help you if you will help us. Our missions are the same."

"Are you faithful to King Saul?"

"No, of course not. Only King Hiram. Saul's battles are not our battles. We are a peaceful seafaring nation. We do not wish to be part of a war. We just want this priestess brought back safe and unharmed."

David nodded and signaled his men to mount up.

"Come! We will make camp up ahead where we will be safe for the night. The Amalekites are like snakes. They come up out of the ground after dark."

Jarib wanted to push on but the officer put his hand up to stop him.

"David is as anxious to get his wives back as you are to bring Laila back. He will know the best way. It is good that we have found him and ride with him. We are all safer, and so will the women be when we find them."

CHAPTER 24

David's men were up well before dawn breaking camp and getting ready to move.

Ishtara and Jarib woke with a start wondering if it was an attack. David stopped close by and heard their question.

"No, we must be ready to move at the first glimmer of daylight. The Amalekites will do the same but they may not know we are pursuing them. I intend to make this the last day of their lives."

"But why did they attack your village and take your people? Were you not all on the same side?"

"No! Amalekites are friends of no one. They were told that I was faithful to King Saul. I was once until Saul attacked me several times and nearly killed me. They have always been enemies of Israel and cause a lot of destruction. Now I will make sure they will not cause any more. I know King Saul will not thank me, but I do this for my people and me, and I will deal with King Saul in God's time."

Quietly they all mounted their horses and started out at a trot until it was light enough to see. When the sky became bright enough, they broke into a gallop through a valley and into the hills beyond. David's scout met them in a pass.

"They are just ahead, still in their camp. That is what they want us to think. When we attack their camp, which has only the women and servants, they will come down out of the north hills and surround us."

The Phoenician officer looked doubtfully at Ishtara and Jarib.

"Perhaps we should go back to Gaza and wait where you will be safe."

Ishtara rode up to the officer and looked him in the eye.

"We will not go back! We have come this far and we will see this to the end, whatever that end may be! You may return with our thanks if you wish."

"No, I cannot. I will continue. King Hiram would have my head if something happened to any of you. Better I should die here."

David and his men were in a huddle mapping out a plan. Five hundred of David's men would go around to the back of the hills and come up behind them. The other hundred with David in the lead would pretend to attack the encampment as a distraction. The five hundred would rush down and fall on the Amalekites from behind and kill them all.

The officer was still very worried but ready to help and approached David.

"What about us?"

"You will come with me. You cannot hide anywhere alone because we do not know if they are all together or some guards are posted around the other side of the camp. You have a better chance of surviving if you stay with us."

David gave knives to Ishara and Jarib.

"I pray God you will not have to use these, but they will save your lives if you do. Please do not hesitate to use them. The Amalekites will rush at you yelling their war cry. Their only thought is to carve you to pieces."

Ishtara remembered the training that Laila had given her so long ago on how to physically defend herself. Laila said she must remain alive to do her work. Ishtara was surprised at how powerfully that training came back to her. She could feel her muscles tense and her body take a posture ready for combat.

David's five hundred men were already on their way around to the back of the hills. They left their horses in a dense thicket and proceeded on foot up through the dense brush. The hundred with David got into position to launch a fake attack and waited for a signal. Jarib kept close to Ishtara.

It seemed an eternity before the signal finally came. Only David knew that whistle. He and his men started forward on the trot and shouted a war cry. Then they galloped toward the encampment. A roar rose to a crescendo from the hills as David's men fell on the Amalekites. The fighting in the hills around them was fierce. David, Ishtara, Jarib, and the officer dismounted and cautiously moved into the camp looking for the women.

Ishtara ran past the men calling to Laila. But the noise of battle was so loud she was sure Laila would not hear her. Once in the camp they discovered that it was empty. They scoured the area for signs of the women but there were none.

After a few hours David's men came down from the hills, bloody and wounded, but victorious. Ishtara and Jarib helped attend to the wounded while David and some of his unwounded men went to look for his wives and Laila.

After several hours David and his men came back leading the horses with the women and servants. They looked bedraggled but unhurt. David came up to Ishtara laughing.

"This priestess of yours helped them all to escape in the night, found a small village in the hills north of here and the villagers hid them! The villagers recognized my wife, Abigail, and her generosity to them a few years ago when they were in need, and were happy to hide and take care of them."

Ishtara thanked David profusely, ran to Laila and threw her arms around her. Jarib hugged the both of them and led them back to where the officer was waiting. Jarib was most relieved of all. Everyone was safe.

"Laila, how did you get away? Amalekites are vicious!"

"They thought we would be too afraid to do anything, so they did not guard us. Just one man stood guard and he was drinking something and falling asleep. I walked up behind him and hit him over the head with a rock as hard as I could. David's wife, Abigail, knew where the village was beyond the hills and guided us there.

"It was difficult in the dark, but a guard from the village lit a small fire to warm himself and we were guided to it by the fire. Abigail recognized him as the son of a woman she had saved from the attack of a wild animal. He went to the village to get help for us. They put us in a small hut, covered us with blankets and then branches. After what seemed an eternity, Abigail heard David's voice shouting her name and we were rescued."

The Phoenician officer looked very relieved to see them.

"Now we shall go back to Gaza and find you a ship to take you back to Tyre, and King Hiram will not have my head after all."

They camped overnight on the way back, which gave Ishtara, Laila, and Abigail time to share more of their life experiences. They were shocked at Abigail's marriage to a nasty drunk who had endangered her people by refusing to give food to David's men. She told how she saved her farm by braving the possibility of being killed, going to David with food for his men and apologies for how her husband had insulted them. The husband was so enraged that he died within a few days. Later on David remembered Abigail and came for her.

Laila apologized for her life seeming so quiet with no dramatic story to tell. But Abigail and the other servants were fascinated to learn what their lives were like in the service of Astarte and life in the temple. Ishtara told how she had come to Gaza in search of her mother's story and what she had learned. Reluctantly they bid each other fond farewells as David and his men, wives and servants prepared to turn back toward the north east.

All four were happy to at last arrive in Gaza the next day. Hannibal was overjoyed to see them and ushered them into his inn. The officer went immediately to his office on the dock to report their success to his superiors.

They ate and talked and ate and talked, and nearly fell asleep at the table. Servants helped them to their rooms and onto their beds. They were asleep immediately.

In the morning they awakened late when the sun was up. The servants brought fresh tunics, sandals and robes and helped them bathe. Refreshed they went to the dining room to break their fast together and continue their discussion of all that happened. They felt so fortunate to find David and his men, and Laila was happy she escaped in the night with David's people and a safe place was found for them all. She and Abigail, David's wife became fast friends and promised to pray for each other, Abigail to Yahweh and Laila to Astarte.

The officer from the dock arrived at the inn to inform them that a ship would leave in the late morning tomorrow to take them to Tyre. Laila and Ishtara jumped up from the table.

"Wonderful! We will have this afternoon to go to the market places to see all their wares from everywhere in the world and to be among the Philistine Gazans."

Hannibal's eyebrows shot up. He hurried to their table.

"You would go out after all you have been through? You must be very careful! This is still Gaza and David is not here to protect you!"

Ishtara and Laila were not to be deprived of this pleasure of going to the market place. Laila had wanted to do that since seeing the markets at Tyre. Ishtara turned to Hannibal.

"It was not the Philistines who took Laila, nor did they attack us in any way. It was Amalekites and they are all dead!"

Jarib looked at Hannibal and just shook his head.

"To the market we will go and, Yahweh and Astarte willing, we will return safe."

CHAPTER 25

Ishtara and Laila found the market and the people fascinating. They were able to communicate with the women who knew Phoenician or spoke a dialect that had shared words. They went from stall to stall exclaiming over the variety of silks and foods, and other exotic items they could not readily identify.

The story about the Amalekites was known by a few and a woman begged them to tell her all about it. The women crowded around Ishtara and Laila to hear about David and his men. He was a folk hero even though he had fallen out of favor with the Philistines from time to time.

Jarib was a little concerned, so he kept watch from a short distance. He could see that Ishtara and Laila had them all enchanted with stories and woman talk. He could not blame them. After all she had him enchanted from the first time he saw her.

The merchants and women gave them many gifts to take back to Phoenicia and baskets in which to carry them. They wanted to refuse them, but it would have broken the people's hearts, so they graciously accepted. The women hugged and kissed Ishtara and Laila wherever they went. It was truly the love of Astarte that shone all about.

It was time to go back to Hannibal's inn for dinner and some rest before the voyage tomorrow. Laila fervently hoped she would not be sick on the ship this time. They bid the women in the market place farewell and walked with Jarib back to the Temple of Dagon and the inn.

Hannibal met them at the door wringing his hands.

"I was so worried about you! I was afraid someone would take you again!"

Ishtara patted his arm.

"The people here are wonderful. We had such a good time talking to them and they loved us. They wanted to hear our story and they gave us baskets of gifts. We did not know that David is their hero!"

"On, no!"

Hannibal clapped his hands to the sides of his head and walked into the inn.

Their dinner was long and quiet. They were thinking about what they would do when they got back home. Ishtara was the only one in danger from King Saul. She and Jarib would go to Endor. Laila would go back to the Temple of Astarte.

"Perhaps King Hiram can deliver us back to Endor."

"Oh, no! I do not care to go up in that swinging basket again! I will take the Secret Way back to the Temple of Astarte, thank you. You two can take the basket."

They awakened in the morning to the loud ringing of Dagon's temple bells. The servants hurried in to help them with their baths and into fresh clothes.

Jarib was curious about them and asked Hannibal, who was just coming into the inn with an arm load of fresh fruit.

"Why did we not hear these bells our first morning here?"

"Oh, there is a celebration of the birthday of Dagon. Every year they ring the bells. I am glad it is only one day. They awaken my guests and often frighten them."

The officer came for them after their breakfast. Hannibal had suggested that Laila eat lightly before the voyage and take a potion with her in case she again became ill.

A small carriage delivered them to the dock and to the ship, Barekbaal. Once again Ishtara was grateful that their boarding would be easy. The captain who greeted them was the same captain who brought them from Tyre. It was good to see a familiar face and the same ship.

They boarded and were escorted up the stairs to the captain's quarters on the upper deck. Everything had been prepared for their comfort. The ship's rowers backed the ship away from the dock and turned it out toward the sea. The sails were hoisted and they were under way toward the shipping channel and Tyre.

The captain told them the trip would take more time because they were going against the prevailing winds and the rowers would be working most of the way. It would mean slower going.

Laila was a little jittery but it was not sea sickness, just nerves. She took some of the potent Hannibal had given her and felt calmer, but decided to stay in the cabin.

Ishtara became quiet and pensive. Jarib wanted to know what she was thinking about. They walked out on deck after the sails were up and watched the shore disappearing behind them.

"I am thinking that I felt safer chasing the Amalekites with David and his men than I will getting back home to Endor."

"You will not be alone again, Ishtara. I will be with you constantly and so will Rébekah and the town's people of Endor. We will get through this together."

"I wish I knew when the pursuit of me will end and how it will end. Will King Saul ever stop looking for me to kill me? How could that happen? One of us must be dead to end it!"

"If that is true, it will not be you, Ishtara. Please do not torture yourself trying to see the future. Let us just walk through it day by day together, whatever comes before us. We will pray, I to Yahweh and you to Astarte. We will be guided and protected, I am sure. Samuel taught me this day by day as we walked the land, through friends or enemies. He walked with courage, in assurance that his god was with him every step of the way. He knew he would not die until his tasks were completed and neither will you."

The thought of Samuel almost brought tears to Ishtara's eyes. She remembered all he told her and the sweetness of their friendship. She wished he were still here so she could tell him everything about their journey. She felt so much stronger now remembering that he was with her in spirit.

"Ishtara, I know what your tears are about. Samuel is always with us as he promised. Life is eternal and we are always one in spirit. We are never separated except by the physical body. Even then we are connected."

She wiped her eyes with her sleeve. Laila eventually came out of the cabin. The breeze blew her hair and robes into a swirl around her. She was smiling and came to join them.

"Are you well, Laila?"

"I am well, Jarib, steady as a rock. Now I can at least enjoy the trip. Ishtara, are you all right? You look sad."

"Yes, I am fine. We were just talking about Samuel and the memories always touch my heart."

The captain joined them and inquired how they were doing.

"The waves will become quite choppy the farther north we go. You may want to stay in the cabin when that happens. The ship will rock and sometimes the spray will make the deck wet and slick. You can lose your footing if you are not used to it. We are not expecting storms, but if you stay on deck and a squall comes up suddenly, be sure to hold onto the mast or ropes as tight as you can. The sailors will get you and pull you up into the cabin."

Laila and Ishtara were sure they would be back in the cabin at the first sign of choppy waters. Jarib enjoyed staying on deck and helping the sailors. He had learned some things from them about sailing and ship riggings on their trip from Tyre and was eager to learn more.

The sea was choppy but there were no squalls to threaten their safety. Ishtara and Laila stayed in the captain's cabin for most of the way. They enjoyed the time together alternately talking and snoozing on the soft pillows. Jarib stayed on deck with the sailors, looking in on Ishtara and Laila from time to time.

The setting sun was beautiful on the water when they arrived in Tyre. The dock was lined with torches and the captain had the sailors light torches on the bow, sides, and stern of the ship. Docking the ship was magical in the torch light against the darkening sky.

Ishtara, Laila, and Jarib bid farewell to the captain, thanking him for his hospitality. They stepped onto the dock and walked to King Hiram's carriage waiting to take them back to the huge inn where they stayed before their voyage. They sat down for a late dinner while their bodies stopped rocking with the sea swells.

CHAPTER 26

They asked the inn keeper if he heard what was happening in Israel.

"My dear guests of King Hiram, King Saul is fighting many battles in the south and east. It is said that the renegade, David, has fought him and could have killed him, but turned away and let King Saul live. Two times he has done this, but King Saul does not recognize that David is not his enemy."

"Do you think we can safely return to the Temple of Astarte?"

"It might be difficult because they do not know where the battles will happen next. They seem to be everywhere."

The inn keeper went to the kitchen to see about preparations there for the next day.

"Jarib, I can go to Endor by the Secret Way, but I cannot take you with me. We must create a joint way and I do not believe you have been taught the skill to safely experience that."

"It is true, Ishtara. That has not been my calling. But I can find my way as a lowly priest of Samuel and Eli. No one will bother me or be looking for me. The local people will warn me if there is trouble or take me in. I will be happy knowing you are safe at Endor and I will join you as soon as I can."

Ishtara sat quietly for a long time while Laila and Jarib chatted and ate the food that was arriving at their table.

"What troubles you, Ishtara?"

"I wanted never to be parted from you, even for a day. But now it seems that must happen for us to get home safely. It will worry me every minute until we are safely together again."

Presently an envoy from King Hiram came to their table.

"The king has ordered a carriage to see you safely to the border of Samaria. From there the wagon that carried you through Samaria will take you back to the valley. Will that be satisfactory?"

"All thanks to Astarte and King Hiram! Yes!"

The envoy bowed and left the inn.

Ishtara burst into tears. The relief from her fears was almost too much. Laila was delighted to continue to travel with them.

"I will ride with you to Samaria and take the Secret Way to the temple from there. I do not look forward to another bumpy ride in that wagon!"

"Ishtara you do not have to go with me through Samaria. You can take the Secret Way any time and I will be happy to suffer the bumpy ride and the swinging basket for you!"

Ishtara burst out laughing.

"I will leave you only if there is no other way to get to Endor, but only if our way is blocked by battles. I do not want to endanger you if King Saul gets word that I am within his reach."

The inn keeper was obviously overhearing them as he went in and out of the dining room.

"The word coming to me from the servants of King Hiram is that King Saul is battling Philistines everywhere and David is pushing the remnant of the Amalekites north and defeating them. David could be battling near the countryside through which you are traveling to return home."

Jarib turned to him and thanked him for the information.

"And what will King Hiram's guards who are with us do if there is a battle near us?"

"They will most likely make a detour through safer territory or leave you in a safe place while they draw attention away from you by returning to Phoenicia."

The three got up from the table and walked outside a short distance from the inn so they could talk privately. Ishtara was very concerned.

"Would they just leave us? Drop us off in a strange place? I know what Laila and I could do. We could create our Secret Way. But what would you do, Jarib?"

"I do not fear this. King Hiram has seen to our needs from the beginning and I do not think we would be in danger that his guards would just abandon us. They will have a plan. I can always make my way to Mount Carmel before we reach Samaria and view any battles from the heights there if they take place in the Jezreel Valley. The priests there will take me in and will have news. When it is safe I will cross and make my way to Endor."

Ishtara was still unsettled about the coming travels and events, but they could only begin the journey and see what would happen. She hated the thought of being separated from Jarib. She would just have to trust that he was clear headed and knew what to do in any event.

They went to their rooms for the night, all sleeping in Ishtara's room. They were deep in thought and sleep seemed illusive. At dawn they got up, bathed in their respective rooms, put on fresh tunics, robes, and sandals, and went to the dining room to break their fast.

The envoy of the king arrived just as they were finishing and announced that the carriage was ready to begin their journey to the Samarian border. His words ran a chill through Ishtara. She still saw it as abandonment, but she was in King Hiram's charge. He had not failed them and she must remember that.

They bid farewell to the inn keeper who had been so gracious and helpful. He wished them the protection of the gods and waved as the carriage lurched forward and rumbled down the road, the horses at a stiff trot.

Ishtara was quiet for a long time, listening to the clip-clop of the horses' hooves and the rumble of the wheels.

"Jarib, I will walk with you to Mount Carmel. Perhaps the driver and guards will take us there instead of Samaria. If they cannot, we can all leave the carriage wherever it stops. I dread the wagon ride and the brigands or soldiers along the roads who might stop and search for us again. It seems so much more ominous this time."

"I agree, Ishtara. It has been on my mind, too. They can take us as far as the port of Akko and we can go on foot to the Mount Carmel monastery from there. Akko is still in Phoenicia. The border is very close after that."

Jarib called to the guard who stopped the carriage. The guard was not happy to change the route that King Hiram had approved, but Jarib convinced him that they had met David near Gaza and helped him rescue his wives and Laila. It would not be difficult for them to find an escort across the valley if all were quiet. He did not mention that Ishtara and Laila would go by the Secret Way. He was sure the guard would not know what he was talking about and think it was sorcery.

Reluctantly the guard agreed after he conferred with the driver and the other guards.

"We will take you just past Akko to our border and you can go from there on foot. I just hope King Hiram does not throw me into the prison or worse."

"You must tell King Hiram that I determined this way was the safest and convey my thanks for all he has done for me in the name of his friendship with Rébekah. He will know what that means."

Ishtara smiled at him and got back into the carriage. She had them stop in Akko and get her a leaf of parchment and a small piece of charcoal colored wax. She wrote a note to King Hiram and gave it to the guard.

"This will tell him what I have told you."

"You can read and write?"

"Yes, I am the High Priestess of Astarte. We learn to read and write, and speak several languages."

The guard looked curiously at the parchment, folded it and placed it under his cuirass.

"I thank you, my lady."

CHAPTER 27

The border of Phoenicia came up quickly after they passed Akko and they disembarked from the carriage. The guard pointed out a path they could take to the bridge over the Kishon River that spills out into the Great Sea. The path would continue up into the mountain to the Carmel Monastery. They bid the guards and the driver farewell with their thanks. They turned to look toward the river and went forward on the barely trodden path, following it to the bridge.

The way was steep and the path wound back and forth, gradually upward. They sat down to rest several times looking out over the Great Sea and then the valley below them until the Carmel Monastery was in sight. The path leveled out as they approached the gate and a monk was present to meet them.

"Jarib, my brother! Welcome! And who are these lovely ladies who courageously navigated the steep path with you?"

Jarib embraced Brother Ammon and turned to introduce Ishtara and Laila.

"Ishtara is the High Priestess and Laila is a senior priestess and teacher at the Temple of Astarte."

"Wonderful! Come! Come in please! You may sit in the garden over here to rest while I gather the brothers from their tasks to come and meet you. Brother Kenan is already coming with refreshments for you."

"Jarib, you are known here?"

"Yes, Laila. Some are from my village and some came here to flee the wrath of King Saul. We are from everywhere in the land, gathered to together to keep the commandments and the teachings, and to live in harmony."

Brother Kenan drew a table up to them and placed the refreshment before them. He did not speak, put his hands together in a prayerful position, bowed and smiled.

"Our brother cannot speak. It was an unfortunate accident in his younger years. However, he does read and write, and cares for our library."

The flower garden reminded Ishtara of the gardens at the Temple of Astarte. The memory tugged at her heart as she realized how much she missed the temple and her life there.

As brother Ammon promised, a parade of monks came from the various buildings and joined together on the central path to come and greet them. He introduced them all by name. Ishtara graciously greeted each one by his name, but she knew she would not be able to remember them all.

"You may refer to each of us as "Brother" as we all do. It is not because we do not remember or value each other's names, but because it reminds us that we are all one in spirit."

Brother Ammon escorted Ishtara and Laila to the guest room while Jarib went among the monks and back to the buildings with them. They showed him their work and talked of their progress in enlarging the monastery buildings and grounds.

The guest room was austere but clean and pleasant. The beds were comfortable but not plush. Light came in through the windows creating a surreal white haze. There was a garden adjacent to the back of the building where they could sit and enjoy the mountain air. It was such a welcome relief from the strong smells of the docks of Tyre, Gaza, and Akko. A short time later Jarib arrived at the guest room.

"The news from the valley is not good right now. There are skirmishes everywhere and King Saul is sending his troops in every direction. The Amalekites came up from the south to escape David and his men. They are trapped between David and King Saul. King Saul tried to use them to fight David, but they were wounded and half dead already.

"Saul sent a local militia, the Ziphites, to trap David on a large hill, while he approached from the other side, but word came that the Philistines were coming, and Saul had to retreat and go back down to fight the Philistines. The local militia used the opportunity to escape from Saul and David, and retreated back to the south, but once David realized that Saul was gone, he went after the Ziphites and killed them all."

David and his men made camp near the Kishon River in the foothills of Mount Carmel. He and a few of his men climbed the mountain and arrived at the gate of the monastery. Brother Ammon opened the gate and welcomed them.

"We do not wish to disturb you or cause you harm brother, but my men are in desperate need of food."

Brother Ammon knew that David's men had done much damage to others who refused to give them food. He bowed graciously and led them up a path and into a cool cave where their food was stored.

"This is our store room and you may take what you need."

David ordered his men to take all they could carry, but not to destroy anything. As they were carrying food from the storage, David turned and saw Ishtara and Laila walking on a path that led toward the chapel. He shaded his eyes to be sure he was seeing correctly. Yes, it was Ishtara and Laila who were at the battle of the Amalekites when he rescued Laila, his wives and servants. He could not mistake Laila's flowing red hair and queenly bearing.

Laila saw David and ran to him. He dropped the bundles of food to embrace her. Then he turned to Ishtara, knelt and kissed her hand.

Jarib came up the path and greeted David warmly. David embraced Jarib and kiss both his cheeks.

"Dear friends! I am so glad we were victorious when I met you and you are all safe and well! How did you manage to get all the way to Mount Carmel through the battles with the Philistines and King Saul?"

"We came by sea on a Phoenician ship, landed in Tyre and took a carriage to Akko and the border of Phoenicia. We walked up the mountain to get there."

David motioned his men to take the food down the mountain while he, Jarib, Ishtara, and Laila sat down together to recount their travels. Laila could not take her eyes off David. He was handsome and so alive. His light brown hair fell in curls over his forehead and his eyes danced as he spoke. Her heart had not responded to any man before now.

She had tried not to think of him on their way to Tyre on the ship, but on the carriage ride she had time to remember and fantasize about him. And now here he was, greeting her with an embrace and spending time with them sitting right across from her. She wanted to talk to him, but words would not come. What could she say? She was a priestess and he was a renegade. Then she heard what he was saying.

"Long before Samuel died he anointed me as the next King of Israel. I was very young when he did the anointing. It has been quite an adventure to keep King Saul from killing me before that can happen. I am sure Samuel knew how this would all come about, but he did not tell me. I had to wait and see for myself."

"Did King Saul know that you were anointed to succeed him as King?"

"I think he did not know about Samuel's anointing, Laila. I think he guessed because I was so successful and he was sure God was with me and God had abandoned him. He said about me, 'What more can he have but the kingdom?'"

"What will you do?"

"I have already proved to Saul that I mean him no harm. Twice I could have killed him while he slept in a cave but I did not. I left him evidence that I had been there during his sleep and did him no harm. But that did not change him. I will continue the battles that must be fought with my six hundred men around me and wait until God makes a way."

Ishtara listened to the conversation with interest. She had told no one that she was Saul's daughter. Only Samuel and Rébekah knew and she felt no compulsion to reveal that now. It would only make them wonder if she were somehow sympathetic to Saul, which she was not.

"Jarib, I need to talk to you alone."

Jarib took Ishtara's arm and they went back to the guest room.

"What is it, Ishtara?"

"I have to tell you something that only Samuel and Rébekah know. King Saul kidnapped and raped my mother. He is my father. That is why he is trying to find me, well not me actually but his daughter who he believes is a sorceress and is putting spells on him to drive him crazy. He does not know my name, but he may begin to think his daughter is connected with the Temple of Astarte. I dare not go back there. It seems I must abandon my beloved temple perhaps forever. I can hardly bear the thought."

CHAPTER 28

David rose to leave and take more food to his men. Some of them were coming back up the mountain to retrieve more food as well. David impulsively turned to Laila.

"I will come back for you, Laila. We must be together."

Laila was shocked out of her fantasy of him.

"But that cannot be! You will be a king and I am a priestess of Astarte, the Phoenician goddess. You must not come for me. I am going back to the temple to continue my duties there. You must fight your battles. I will pray for you but I cannot be with you."

Now David was shocked.

"No woman would ever refuse me! How can you?"

"Please understand, David, it is impossible for me. I am not rejecting you. A priestess takes vows and lives a life very different from other women. I cannot forsake those vows and my dedication to Astarte."

David stood still and contemplated what she said. He wanted to be angry, but he could not.

"I do not understand, but I will honor what you have said."

"Thank you, David. You will always be in my heart and I wish you victory. I will rejoice when you are the King."

His men came out of the cave and they all went back down the mountain. Laila was still in shock. Jarib and Ishtara came from the guest house to where she stood.

"Laila, come. We will go together for dinner. The monks will soon ring the bell and we should not be late."

She smiled at them and followed behind them, still in a daze. David wanted her and she wanted him, but she could not be his in that way.

She had been joyfully contented as a priestess and now her world was thoroughly shaken. She sought out Ishtara after dinner to speak with her alone.

"I had to tell David that he should not come for me. It is impossible for me to be with him because I am a priestess and he will be a king. That I do not live like other women and cannot. Yes, I could leave the temple for him, but then what would I be? He could even discard me and I would be an outcast. I am very confused."

"Laila, you told David what is true. He has many wives and as a king he will have more and you will be little more than a servant to those women. You do not belong in that world. I understand that you are attracted to David. What woman would not be? But that is not your life.

"The attraction might fade with disappointment that you are no longer his passion. And then there is your ability to work with cosmic energies. Others could decide that you are a sorceress and demand that he drive you away or kill you, as my mother was killed by King Saul."

"I see your happiness with Jarib and I think I would like to be happy with someone, too."

"Jarib is a priest, Laila, not a king. He is kind and devoted to our love. He understands the difference between his training and mine, between Yahweh and Astarte. We see our god and goddess as the true divine consorts. They are light and light, not the lower opposites of light and dark. You are light, Laila. You have always lived in the light. David is still in darkness. Some day he may honor the light, but it will be in a different way and in a different world from yours."

"I know you are right, Ishtara. I have been your teacher and now you are mine. I have taught you to focus your mind and be strong, now I must do that very thing that I have taught. I must go back to the Temple of Astarte and remember who I am as her devoted priestess.

"This outer world of intrigue, battle, killing, and hatred creates a powerful fascination when we are touched by it, but it is only that and it is not my reality. I will stay with you and Jarib a while, and when it feels right I will create the Secret Way and return to the temple."

David came back to the monastery to thank the monks for their generosity and promised to protect them should anyone threaten them. He approached Ishtara and Jarib.

"If you ever need me to help you get home or defend you in any other way, please send a message and I will come."

He embraced Jarib and briefly knelt on one knee before Ishtara in honor of her high position. Furtively he glanced around but Laila was nowhere to be seen. Laila had stayed in the guest house until David, disappointed, went back down the mountain. She knew it would not be good to see him again. She would only fall back into agonizing confusion and torture herself with fantasies of being his.

Brother Ammon approached Jarib and Ishtara with an offer to perform a marriage ceremony for them.

"Our ceremony is a spiritual coming together of two people in higher understanding of their relationship and mission in the world together. Laila may perform the ceremony according to the love and teachings of Astarte and I will perform the joining according to the love and teachings of Yahweh. Would this please you and fulfill your desire to be one at all levels of being?"

Ishtara and Jarib smiled at each other and nodded their agreement.

"Brother Ammon, how blessed we are with your offer. We are delighted to accept! Let us get Laila and we can begin to plan the service."

Laila was delighted with the opportunity to plan a service with Brother Ammon and create a wonderful atmosphere in the gardens of flowers. All thoughts of David were whisked out of her mind. She and Brother Ammon picked out a place in the garden, surrounded it with vases of flowers of all kinds and the brothers erected a canopy.

Excitement buzzed through the monastery. It was their first wedding. Each one had a gift to add to the festivities and soon created a beautiful venue. In the cool of the evening, the ceremony began. Gentle breezes were blowing in from the Great Sea, the nearly setting sun was gentle over the waters, and they gathered in quiet joy to witness this holy joining.

Laila and Brother Ammon had planned the ceremonies so they were perfectly in harmony, and they were sure that Yahweh and Astarte were smiling down upon them.

Jarib and Ishtara pledged themselves to each other and to the holiness that surrounded their lives. They all sang and danced, toasted each other with the monastery's special wine and smashed the cups under their feet. Brother Ammon and Laila pronounced them married as husband and wife, and a great cheer went up from the brothers when they sealed their vows with a kiss.

The monks in the kitchen brought out a wonderful banquet of freshly baked breads, sliced meats, figs and fruit. Ishtara was curious.

"Brother Ammon, I thought David's men took all of your stores of food."

"Oh, yes. Well, we have several storage places. They were welcome to take everything in the one we showed them. We knew it would easily supply all of his men. We have plenty for ourselves and guests."

The brothers all gathered around to have conversations with the guests and each other. The evening wore on into darkness and they all bid each other a restful night. Jarib, Ishtara and Laila went back to the guest house.

"I will go back to the temple in the morning. I am so happy I could be part of your ceremony! It was so unexpected. I will give everyone at the temple your good wishes. Abigail will be so happy to hear your news. When I can I will join you at Rébekah's and Abigail, too."

In the morning they quietly broke their fast together and Laila created the Secret Way. They hugged each other and kissed each other's cheeks and then she was gone.

CHAPTER 29

Jarib and Ishtara spent another few weeks at the monastery to enjoy their time as a married couple. They studied with some of the monks in the small library. Jarib helped some of the ones who were building another building. It was a joyful time. Their time with Brother Ammon was enlightening and drew them all closer together.

"I know we must leave. Laila will need me close even though I will not be at the temple. I long to see Abigail again and tell her what I learned in Gaza. I miss the temple, the singing and dancing, and all the young priestesses."

"Tell me when you want to go and I will follow after you. Brother Ammon has a wagon at the bottom of the mountain and a farmer keeps donkeys for him. He has offered to take me across the valley. Two of the brothers will come with us so he does not have to come back alone. He wants to see Samuel's tomb and perhaps meet some of my brother priests. He will drop me off in the valley near Endor.

"What about the Philistines and the battles you might encounter?"

"The shepherds and the local people will know if there are battles in the valley. Word has it that David beat the Philistines back farther to the south and toward the coast. I cannot be in fear and wait here forever to be with you at Endor. My life is not here in this monastery, but in Endor. We have much to do and plans to make for our future work."

They planned to go on the next day. Ishtara did not know how she would tear herself away from Jarib even for a few days, but she knew she must. Rébekah was not getting any younger and would need her there, too.

They spent the night making love and hoping the morning light would not come too soon. Eventually they fell asleep in each other's arms.

Very early in the morning they broke their fast and Ishtara said goodbye to Brother Ammon and the brothers.

"Take good care of my Jarib, Brother Ammon. I would not care to live without him."

"Be at peace, Ishtara. We will go with prayer and Yahweh's good will and protection."

Reluctantly, she created the Secret Way, kissed Jarib, stepped forward and was immediately in Rébekah's circle at Endor.

Before Jarib could feel abandoned and bereft, Brother Ammon touched his shoulder.

"Come. We must get started before the heat of the day is upon us."

They set off down the mountain side and Brother Ammon showed him the cave where the wagon was stored. The four pulled it out and brushed off some of the twigs and dust. The farmer saw them coming with the wagon and met them with the donkeys.

The farmer gave them bread, figs and water and hitched the donkeys.

"They are a bit frisky. They have not had much work to do for me on the farm the last few months. They will be glad for the exercise."

Jarib, Brother Ammon, and two brothers climbed into the wagon, thanked the farmer, and started for the valley. They drove for an hour when three soldiers on horses came galloping up to the wagon.

"Do not show fear, only friendliness. We are just lowly priests going to Samuel's tomb."

"Stop in the name of King Saul! Who are you and where are you going?"

Brother Ammon smiled graciously.

"We are just priests of Eli going to the tomb of Samuel to grieve and pay our respects. Have we strayed from the road to Ramah? Might you tell us if we are going the right way?"

"Yes, this is the way to Ramah if you like rough goat paths!"

They laughed and galloped away.

Jarib had to admit that he was a little shaken, thinking they might be delayed and he would not get to Endor.

A few more hours and they met two of David's scouts in the low hills. They recognized Jarib and came out of hiding to speak with him.

"Have you seen any of Saul's men?"

"Only three. They questioned us briefly and went on their way to the north, probably returning to King Saul's fortress in Gibeah."

"There is a small spring in the hills nearby if you and your animals need water. Come this way."

They discovered there were more than two scouts, but a few hundred of David's men farther into the hills. They watered the donkeys, filled their water skins and started back to where they had met the scouts.

Brother Ammon was a little concerned.

"Do you think they will trust us not to reveal their location?"

"Yes. They know me. Ishtara and I rode with them to rescue Laila and David's wives when we were in Gaza. It was quite an experience. Laila was taken from Dagon's temple by Amalekites after they destroyed David's Village of Ziklag and took his people. A Phoenician officer, Ishtara and I rode out to find her and found David and his six hundred men. We joined them in the hunt and rescue."

They found their way back and started for the valley again. As they got closer to where Jarib would leave Brother Ammon and his brothers, there was the thunder of horses' hooves coming from the south.

"Those are Philistines!"

They pulled the wagon off to the side into a thicket of small trees and waited.

The Philistines passed by at full gallop without noticing them. They were watching for David's men, knowing they must be close by.

"Let us wait a little longer. We do not want to get into the middle of a battle."

They dismounted from the wagon, covered the donkeys' eyes and noses so they would not call out to the other animals, and sat down to wait.

Ishtara went immediately to Rébekah's hut and found an elderly priestess from the Village of Endor coming out.

"My lady, she has been ill but beginning to recover. I am so glad you are here. She has missed you and watches for you every day."

Ishtara kissed her and went in immediately to find Rébekah on her bed sipping a healing potion of tea and herbs. She looked small and fragile. When Ishtara walked in she brightened up.

"Ishtara! I am so glad you have returned. Tell me all about your travels. Where are Jarib and Laila?"

"I will tell you everything. But first, what has happened to you? What is the illness you are suffering?"

"It is just old age, Ishtara. A cough and a pain in my chest, but not very bad. I am healing. So, tell me before I die of anticipation!"

Ishtara told her the whole story from the guards stopping the wagon before they got to Samaria, the ship voyages, the taking of Laila, meeting David and his men, to the wedding at Mount Carmel Monastery.

"A wedding! Your wedding! I wish I could have been there. Where is Jarib now? And Has Laila gone back to the Temple of Astarte? I know I have so many questions, but I have missed so much. I guess age makes you stay put and not adventure about."

"The wedding was beautiful. The brothers at the monastery made us so welcome by creating a place in the garden for it to take place, building a canopy and helping Laila design the lovely ceremony. I, too, wish you could have been there. You would have loved it."

"And did you satisfy your curiosity about Dagon and Ishara?"

"The answer is not as I hoped it might be. I can see that searching in the realm of the gods will not hold an earthly answer. But I could see more clearly how humanity has created that realm searching for a higher purpose for life. The answers are in our cosmic understanding of life eternal, and not in earthly events. I am content."

CHAPTER 30

Laila was happy to be back at the Temple of Astarte. The young priestesses welcomed her with a celebration of dancing and a special picnic out in the gardens. They wanted to know every detail of her travels and were shocked that she had been kidnapped from the Temple of Dagon by the Amalekites. She mentioned only briefly that it was David and his men who rescued her and the other captives. It was still too painful to think about David and their meeting at Mount Carmel.

Abigail came back from a short trip to a village and hurried to greet and hug Laila. She looked deeply into Laila's eyes.

"Something happened, did it not? Come with me. We will sit away from the others and you must tell me everything."

Laila burst into tears. Abigail went to the picnic area and took a flask of wine.

"Drink some of this. It will ease you."

Laila gulped a mouthful, tears running down her cheeks. The wine did quiet her sobs and she began to tell Abigail every detail starting from being lowered in the basket over the cliffs of Endor. The description made Abigail laugh and Laila laughed with her. When she came to the part of meeting David at Mount Carmel and his proposal she began to tear up a little.

"I told him all the reasons that it could not be, but in the power and excitement of his presence, it sounded so trivial, like excuses made up by a frightened little girl."

"Who we are and how we live as priestesses is not easy to explain to anyone who has no understanding of the spiritual nature. It can sound naïve and childish."

"Ishtara had a long talk with me that helped me get centered in my truth again. I was her teacher and now she is mine. Ishtara and Jarib's wedding took place at the monastery and that helped me forget David and be excited to plan the ceremony."

"We are always teaching each other, Laila. We can be both teacher and student without feeling shame that we are not at the top of the spiritual mountain all the time. Tell me about the wedding!"

Jarib and the brothers waited for several hours until it seemed that everything was quiet. The troops were gone and David's men were far behind them. They took the hoods off the donkeys' heads and hitched them to the wagon. They cautiously rolled out of the thicket and turned toward the valley and Endor again.

"They are all most likely heading for King Saul's fortress in Gibeah, Saul's soldiers, David, and the Philistines. That will be the battle to end all battles!"

Jarib agreed. He was eager to get to Endor and Ishtara before anything more could happen.

"You will need to be long gone from here. You can leave me anywhere and return home by another route. Perhaps visiting Samuel's burial place in Ramah is a good idea. It might be the safest place."

"We will take you as far as we can, Jarib. If we are stopped again, we can still say that we got lost on trying to find a road to Ramah. Ishtara would never forgive me if something happened to you because I dumped you in the middle of a battle ground."

It was slow going through rocky places and hills with no apparent passage through the brush. They got out of the wagon several times and pushed it, with Brother Ammon leading the donkeys, urging them forward.

The valley floor eventually became smoother and Jarib could see the cliffs of Endor in the distance.

"Brother Ammon, would you like to come with me to meet Rébekah? We can hide the wagon and donkeys in Samuel's hermitage cave that is not too far from here. You and the brothers could spend the night in Endor and start for Ramah in the morning. The people of the Village of Endor have protected Rébekah and her place on the cliffs for many years. They will welcome her guests."

The brothers talked together and decided they would like to visit Endor and Rébekah.

"How do we get there?"

They put the wagon in the cave and hobbled the donkeys so they could graze. Jarib led them up the winding goat path to the bottom of the cliff. He pulled on a vine that rang a bell at the top and called out the pass words, "Samuel brings a guest!"

They sat at the bottom of the cliff for an hour when they heard the bumping and thumping of the basket being lowered down the cliff wall. Jarib reached out and guided the basket to the ground.

"We will go two at a time. The men at the top will bring us up. It is slow but better than walking many miles around the mountain to find the path through a thick forest. Brothers, please step in."

Brother Ammon and another brother gingerly stepped into the basket. The vines began to groan and the basket creaked. The brothers looked up and then back at Jarib as if to say, 'are you sure.'

When they were all at the top, the basket was stowed and the men disappeared into the path to the village. Jarib guided the brothers on the path that led to Rébekah's home.

Ishtara rushed out to greet them and ran into Jarib's arms. Rébekah hobbled out right behind her and threw her arms around Jarib. Ishtara introduced the monastery brothers and Rébekah was delighted. She hugged them all. Whatever had been Rébekah's affliction, seemed to have been healed in the joy of the reunion and the wonderful visitors from Mount Carmel.

Ishtara drew Rébekah aside.

"We have something to tell you Rébekah. I am with child, I am sure. Majah came to me in a dream and said that I am to have a child!"

"Ishtara and Jarib, come with me to the Sacred Circle. There must be a blessing called down for you!"

Because Rébekah was becoming frail, she took the Secret Way to the Sacred Circle. They all sat down together and Rébekah explained to Jarib who the cosmic mothers were.

She began a chant to call the cosmic mothers to gather for the blessing.

"Yes, Ishtara you are to have two children, twins."

Jarib looked surprised and amazed.

"Two? Are you sure?"

"The cosmic mothers are never wrong, Jarib. They see souls and if they say there are two, then there are two. They will be born very soon. And a daughter will follow after them within a short time."

While Ishtara and Jarib lingered to take in the news, Rébekah took the Secret Way back to her hut. She was exhausted and laid down on her bed.

The elderly priestesses knew that Rébekah would be unable to prepare a dinner. They came from the village bringing food and busied themselves preparing the dinner for all of them.

The brothers accompanied the priestesses back to the Village of Endor where they would be guests for the night.

They spent the evening all sharing stories and wine. Their laughter could be heard echoing off the distant hills.

Early in the morning the whole village was awakened by the tromping of soldiers' feet. There were only two of them. They demanded in the name of King Saul to know if the woman, Rébekah lived there.

The priestesses met them and kindly offered to assist them. First they offered them refreshment, wine and figs. The soldiers gratefully accepted the hospitality, looked around a bit, and then followed the priestesses into the wooded path toward Rébekah's hut. The brothers were right behind them. Half way there the soldiers dropped to the ground.

"Are they dead?"

"No, just asleep for the rest of the day. Gather them up and bring them to the cliff to the basket."

The brothers and priestesses lugged them the rest of the way past Rébekah's hut and toward the cliff edge.

Jarib and Ishtara came out of the hut and saw the parade going past. Brother Ammon announced that they would take them in the wagon to Ramah and drop them off in a small village where they would not know where they were, or even who they were for the rest of the day. He bid them all god speed, picked up his share of the burden, and trudged on.

They were all lowered over the cliff in the basket two at a time. The unconscious soldiers were carried down the winding goat path to the wagon in Samuel's cave. They hitched the donkeys and slowly drove away down into the valley and to the south.

CHAPTER 31

King Saul was tortured day and night by fear that this daughter was surely somewhere in his kingdom casting spells on him to get revenge for the murder of her mother. He had tried to tell Samuel about his fears, but Samuel would never listen to him.

"Just be faithful to God and do what God decrees. Your fears are baseless. God is protecting the faithful! See that you are one of them."

The servants could hear Saul raging in his quarters and throwing objects, smashing urns, and tearing draperies. They ran and hid behind the great kitchen hearths until a guard would come to say that all was quiet. They were terrified that Saul would summon them and throw things at them, too, or slay them as he had tried to do to David the harpist.

Now with Samuel dead, Saul did everything he could think of to hear from God. The great battle with the Philistines was on the horizon. They were nearing Saul's fortress and Saul was in a panic. He needed answers from God. Even the Urim and Thummim, the priestly oracle for divining the will of God, did not work for him. No symbols, chants, or pleadings made any difference. There was only deadly silence from God, only the gentle flapping of the tent roof.

"Guards! Guards!"

The guards came running and bowed before Saul.

"Has a sorceress, a woman with a spirit, been found yet? I need her to bring up the spirit of Samuel that he may tell me what to do! All of Israel is in danger!"

"Not yet, Sire. Our people are out looking everywhere. The women accused have been killed or fled the country."

"Fools! Keep looking! The Philistines will be upon us! Go!"

The guards bowed, backed out of King Saul's presence, and ran down the halls to the servants' quarters. Malachi met them half way to the gate of the fortress.

"Come with me quietly."

They went to Malachi's hut on the hill behind the prison where they could secretly discuss where they might find such a woman or what to do next.

"Even if we do find her, King Saul will surely have her killed! She would endanger her life by admitting to being a sorceress or allow that Saul should be brought to her. She should flee the country!"

Malachi shuddered as he remembered well what Saul did to Majah and this might bring him dangerously close to Ishtara. Ishtara looked so much like Majah now, that Saul would certainly guess who she was and murder her immediately.

"What does he want with the woman?"

"God will not speak to him and he demands that we find a woman with a spirit to conjure up dead Samuel. He wants Samuel to tell him what will happen in the next battle with the Philistines. He is desperate!"

Malachi rubbed his beard and thought for a few minutes.

"Take two trusted servants with you and go secretly to the Village of Endor. The residents will direct you to Rébekah. Tell her I sent you and ask her what to do. She will know. Keep sending the other servants among the population to look for a woman with a spirit, but tell them not to question anyone. They should look throughout the land to fulfill the king's order, but be sure not to find anyone."

Rébekah sensed the crackle of footsteps of the servants coming through the back woods toward Endor. They stopped in the Village of Endor to inquire about Rébekah, but no one would speak to them. The villagers turned away and disappeared into their homes. When they mentioned the name Malachi, an elderly priestess pointed at the pathway. They walked quietly through the wooded path.

Rébekah stepped into the path and confronted them.

"Who are you and what do you want?"

The servants were shocked at Rébekah's sudden appearance before them. They shrank back for a moment. Then they knelt before her in honor of her friendship with Malachi.

"We have come from Malachi, my lady. Please, there is great danger."

"Say no more. Come with me."

They followed her as she hobbled through the woods to the Sacred Circle above the cliffs and nervously sat down on the benches at her bidding.

"We are safe here. Now, tell me. What danger are you speaking of?"

"King Saul is demanding that we find a sorceress to conjure up the ghost of Samuel. He seeks Samuel's advice about the coming battle with the Philistines. He rants and shouts that God will not listen to him. That he needs Samuel."

Rébekah's graying eyebrows shot up and her toothless mouth dropped open.

"Conjure the ghost of Samuel? Holy Astarte! He must believe that someone can actually do that!"

Dismayed, she sat down on the bench with the servants.

"It has long been a myth among the people who wish to see their deceased loved ones again, but it is not true. Magicians take their money and use evil tricks to make them believe they have seen them. I do not believe in this, but if indeed the dead can return for some reason, it is surely their choice! They cannot be forced or dragged up out of their tombs."

Rébekah paused for a long time thinking. The servants sat quietly looking at the ground and trying not to fidget, but they were nervous.

"It is true we can go into the cosmic realms to commune with those who have passed on, but we do not yank their bodies or souls out of the ground! In the cosmic realms there is no verbal communication. We are not given advice by them or predictions of the future."

She closed her eyes and thought a while longer.

"Please, my lady, King Saul will imprison and kill us and our families if we do not obey his command to find and bring him to a sorceress. We believe you have spoken the truth, but he will not listen to us. What can we do?"

The servants looked nervously at each other and wrung their hands. Rébekah looked at them compassionately. She knew the trouble they were in if they failed to fulfill Saul's demands.

"You must go back and tell the king that you can bring him to a sorceress only at the full moon. Do not mention my name or Endor, but only as a woman with a spirit. That will give me time to prepare. Go to Malachi first. He will know how to tell the king without endangering all of you."

Rébekah gave them bread and figs, blessed them, and sent them on their way back to Malachi.

King Saul had not eaten or slept in days and was elated at the news that a woman with a spirit had been found. He did not want anyone to know that the king would go to a sorceress, so he disguised himself in traveler's clothing and took two guards with him who were sworn to secrecy upon pain of death. He was weak from lack of nourishment so they took an ass from his stables and helped him to mount it.

At the full moon an hour before midnight, the servants led the two guards and King Saul by a circuitous way around Endor so they wouldn't know where they were going. They avoided Rébekah's hut and came through the woods to the Sacred Circle a short distance from the edge of the cliff.

Rébekah, Ishtara, and Jarib were waiting in the shadows. They had built a fire in the middle of the Sacred Circle that cast eerie images all about. The servants helped Saul dismount and disappeared back into the wooded darkness with the ass. Saul motioned the two guards to stay back while he went forward alone. He looked wildly around at the benches and fire.

"Where is the sorceress?"

CHAPTER 32

Rébekah stepped up near the fire light where Saul could see her. Her robe was blowing in the breeze and her gray hair hung down close to her face. She stood there for a few minutes allowing Saul to take in the whole ghostly scene. He was shaking and wide eyed.

"What is it that you want of me?"

"I want you to conjure up the spirit of a man I shall name! Are you the sorceress?"

"Surely you know that King Saul has driven all the wizards and sorcerers from the land. Why then do you come to me? Are you plotting my death?"

"As the Lord lives, I will not allow you to be harmed."

"Who do you want brought up from the dead?"

He dropped to his knees before her, arms outstretched.

"Samuel! Bring me Samuel! I need Samuel. God is angry with me and will not answer me. God is silent to me but he will speak to Samuel! I must know about the outcome of the coming battle with the Philistines! Will I be victorious or will I not and we will all die?"

"Give me a moment to prepare myself."

As Rébekah stepped back into the shadows Ishtara, who now looked exactly like her mother, stepped into the flickering light of the fire. Saul looked up at her in horror as she spoke.

"You are King Saul, are you not? You are the one who took me from my temple and raped me!"

"What? Majah? No! No! It cannot be you! You are dead! Go away!"

"Yes, it is I. You had me declared a sorceress and sent me to the prison where you ordered my death. I was never a sorceress and you knew that! Your god will not forgive you for that lie and will never speak to you."

Saul threw himself face down on the ground and cried out.

"You are dead! Where is the real sorceress? I demand that she bring me Samuel! Bring me Samuel!"

Ishtara tossed something into the fire that created a rising blue haze all around them and then backed into the shadows. Jarib stepped to the edge of the fire light wearing a white robe and knowing that Samuel was always with him, he spoke in Samuel's voice.

Saul put his forehead on the ground and closed his eyes. He was so desperate that he believed he heard the angry voice of Samuel saying exactly what he feared.

"Why are you disturbing me when even God will not answer you? Tomorrow you and Jonathan will die in battle and you will be with me! Now leave me in peace."

Saul rose on one elbow looking up, reached out his hand toward the fire, and began gasping for breath.

"No, Samuel! I beg of you! No! No!"

Jarib disappeared back into the shadows and stood beside Ishtara.

After a short time Rébekah came to stand by Saul and motioned to his two companions to come, lift him from the ground and bring him to her hut. In anguish he wanted to break free and run, but she stopped him.

"No, stay and eat. You have no strength. You have not eaten for days! I will prepare a meal for you to nourish you."

He wanted to object, but indeed he had no strength even for that. He leaned heavily on his guards and obeyed her.

She prepared meat and bread. She fed him with figs, the wine, the bread and meat. He fell asleep for a short time and awakened when he was somewhat revived to see her standing by him.

"You see, Saul. I am just a weak old widow woman, cooking food for you as any mother would do. I have no spirits. I do not know what you believe you saw here, but nothing has happened.

"You called out for Majah and Samuel, but neither of them were here. Only you and I and your guards were here. Perhaps it was your lack of food for several days that caused a delusion to rise up in your mind. Now go in peace knowing that Yahweh will be with you."

The servants reappeared with the ass, helped Saul mount it, and guided the three back to Saul's fortress. It was doubtful that any of the three would know just where they had been or what had transpired.

Saul's worst fears had spoken to him. Still terrified, dazed, and confused by the experience, he could tell no one about it. Immediately he ran to the encampment to his troops. It was the only place where he felt strong and sure of himself. He was relieved that they were all waiting there and expecting him. His generals gathered about him and began to speak of their battle plans.

They believed that David was still fighting the Amalekites in the south and driving north, but he had already vanquished the Amalekites. Young David who had fled from King Saul's wrath now had a small but victorious army of his own. Saul knew this and was enraged. Wherever he went the people were chanting.

"Saul has slain his thousands, but David has slain his ten thousands!"

"Saul has slain his thousands, but David has slain his ten thousands!"

He could not go after David in battle again because he was beset by the Philistines on several fronts. He had chased David and his men up onto a mountain side and had them trapped until a messenger came and with the news that the Philistines were right behind them. He was forced to turn from pursuing David and fight off the Philistines. David knew that God had saved him again and fell to his knees giving thanks, and Saul knew it too.

The Philistine fires could be seen in the distance at night surrounding Saul's fortress. Their taunting shouts echoed in the hills. Saul's men could see the Philistine torches moving about and feared that spies were watching their every move. Saul and his generals were awake all night making feverish last minute plans, knowing that the Philistines would come at dawn.

The next morning the Philistines came running in massive numbers and the battles were everywhere around them. Saul's troops tried to meet them on every front, but there were too many. The battles lasted all day until Saul was finally defeated, and Saul and his son, Jonathan, lay dead in the fields.

With the Ziphites now utterly destroyed, David and his men turned and started back toward the valley. They were not far from Gibeah. His spies reported that the Philistines were headed for Saul's fortress and David mobilized his small army in that direction immediately.

"Maybe now King Saul will understand that I am not his enemy. We will fight beside him in the battle that is coming."

But David was too late. The battle was over by the time he got there and the Philistines were overrunning the fortress. The servants and Malachi had fled the night before. In the hills David and his men stood by helplessly. They knew they could not pursue the Philistines alone.

At the news of the deaths of Saul and Jonathan, David mourned Jonathan who had been his closest and dearest friend, and had saved him from Saul's wrath many times.

Word spread throughout the country that King Saul and his son Jonathan were both killed in battle and the Philistines had gone. In the streets and countrysides, the people hailed David as their new king. Then he knew it was time to step forward to take his place, anointed by Samuel and ordained by God as King David. He and his men went to Hebron, as God directed him, where he was declared king over the house of Judah.

CHAPTER 33

Laila heard the news at the Temple of Astarte. She was happy for David that his dream of being the king had come true. Again she was reminded of how impossible any coming together between them would always be. This reality again tugged at her heart and set her dreams afire for him.

Ishtara came to the Temple of Astarte knowing that Laila would appreciate her support. She was mortified to hear that Saul's head was cut off and his headless body was hung on a city wall.

In the night the victorious Philistines had deposited his armor outside the gate of the Temple of Astarte. Ishtara hung back. She was aghast at the bloody sight of the mangled armor and puzzled as to why it was here. Why would this be brought to the Temple of Astarte of all places?

Abigail and Laila took Saul's armor in, cleaned it, and put it in a small chapel behind the main building.

"Abigail, why are we keeping his armor here? Saul was so destructive to Majah and to me. Will this not further displease his god? Must we honor him this way?"

"The Philistines did this to dishonor Saul, claiming victory for their god Dagon. They do not know that we keep the high watch for Astarte as a friend of Yahweh, who can never be defeated.

"Come sit down with me, Ishtara, and I will tell you and Laila both the story of the hapless miserable Saul."

Laila took Ishtara's hand and they sat down close together.

"The people were demanding that Samuel appoint a king over them. They were fearful and wanted a king to fight their battles for them. Samuel told the people the terrible things that would happen to them if they had a king ruling over them. He said they would be heavily taxed, their sons and daughters would be conscripted into the military or taken into slavery. He would take the best of their family, animals and goods into his service. The best of their crops and vineyards would be taken from them. But the people refused to listen to Samuel.

"Samuel said, 'Because of your king whom you chose for yourselves, you will cry out and the Lord will not answer you in that day.'

"Saul was a tall and handsome young man of the tribe of Benjamin, who was out in his father's field where he was plowing. His father's asses wandered away and Saul went looking for them. He paid a prophet to help locate them which was customary. God told Samuel to go to Saul and anoint him. It was a surprise to Saul. He did not even know what being anointed meant, but he followed Samuel's further instructions.

"Samuel called the tribes together and they cast lots to elect Saul as their King. Saul was terrified and certainly not willing to be a king. He knew nothing about being a king. He was a simple farm boy. Desperately he ran and hid from them among the camel baggage, but they found him and crowned him king right there.

"And so he was forced to be the king. Since then he lived a life of war and fear that he did not choose. He was scolded by Samuel for his ineptness, his disobedience, and was afraid of God. He is your father, Ishtara, and we will protect his spirit until his god chooses to purify him. Even though he did great harm to us, by keeping his armor secured in the chapel behind the temple, we act in love and the darkness of Ba'al will not be able to trespass on the Temple of Astarte again.

"I am sorry, Abigail, but I will never go near where his armor is kept. I do not wish to be reminded of him. I will leave the Temple of Astarte now and go to Rébekah for counsel."

Laila was shocked at all that was transpiring.

"But you are the High Priestess, Ishtara! You cannot just leave us! What will we do?"

Ishtara took both of Laila's hands and sat down with her in the garden.

"It is within my power to appoint another High Priestess in my place and I appoint you, Laila. We will arrange for your ceremony today and begin as soon as all is made ready."

"I understand and I am willing, but losing you is a terrible price."

Laila's eyes were full of tears. They held each other and wept together. Ishtara sent a young priestess to gather all that was needed. A place for Laila to spend the week in seclusion was made ready and Laila entered it. Ishtara tended to her needs throughout the time, and helped her bathe and dress in the ceremonial vestments.

The young priestesses began the dance as Laila was led through them to the altar of flowers. Ishtara repeated the sacred ritual blessing as Abigail had done for her.

"The priestess becomes the High Priestess when she has the knowledge, experience, desire, and ability to give of herself to be of service to others and to the Divine. Laila, you have fulfilled these requirements and attained this high office. You have agreed to fulfill the duties of this high office. I declare now that you are a High Priestess of the Temple of Astarte. May you be forever blessed as you walk a new path in high consciousness and joy!"

As Ishtara had done at her ceremony, Laila prayerfully took the golden chalice from Ishtara. Tears were running down her cheeks as she kissed it, lifted it in devotion to Astarte, and placed it on the altar among the flowers. Music from the harps and golden bells infused the air. Then dancing stopped at the signal from Ishtara. The dancers knelt and sang a blessing, closing the service.

"Laila, you are now the High Priestess of the Temple of Astarte. Someday I may return, if it is right, and we will be together as we have always worked together. You will be in my heart and I will be ready to help if you need me."

They went to the dining room where the young priestesses were singing and laughing. They sat down to eat and enjoyed the merriment that had always been part of their experience.

They went out to the garden to pray together. Then Ishtara created the Secret Way for herself and Abigail, and they arrived immediately at Rébekah's place on the cliffs of Endor.

Laila went to the highest point of the hill on which the temple sat and looked out across the valley. It was a lonely moment, as if everything in her life just fell away and she was alone. Ishtara and Abigail were at Endor with Rébekah but would eventually return.

The breezes of the evening tugged at her hair and robe, and the coolness felt refreshing on her tear dampened cheeks. The sun was setting in the west and it seemed as though the sun were setting on her former life as well.

"Mistress, someone is at the gate asking for you!"

The young priestess was wide-eyed, not knowing exactly what to do. It was then that Laila realized she needed to train and elevate some of them to assist her and help her run the affairs of the temple.

"Who is as the gate, Anah? Did they give a name?"

"Yes, Mistress, he said his name is David."

Laila's knees nearly gave away.

"Are you sure he said that his name is David?"

"Yes, Mistress and there are many soldiers with him. But they are a little farther away, not close to the gate. He is alone at the gate."

Trying to steady herself, she walked down the hill toward the temple gate. There he was, resplendent in all his kingly glory. She could barely catch her breath. She reached for the gate for support, but did not open it.

"Laila! I hope my coming here does not distress you. I just had to see you again."

"I am High Priestess Laila now and how do I address you? Your Highness the King? Your Majesty?"

"Please Laila, High Priestess of Astarte, call me David as you did on Mount Carmel."

"David, this is distressing me very much. Why are you here?"

"I want to talk to you, to tell you what has happened to me, and to be your friend."

"No, I cannot do this. I do not know what you want other than what you said on Mount Carmel. I have already explained the impossibility to you. There is nothing more I can say."

"Please, trust that I will not say those things again. Anything you need, please call upon me and I will help you. I will see that your temple is protected and that no one threatens you in any way."

Slowly Laila pushed the gate open and allowed David to step in. She showed him to a bench in the nearby garden and they sat down together. She looked into his mind for a moment and saw no guile there.

"David, the last time a king came to this gate, or sent his guards, Ishtara's grandmother, who was the High Priestess was grabbed, thrown into a chariot and carried away to be brutally raped by Saul. When there was news that she was pregnant, he condemned her as a sorceress and had her murdered in the dungeon of his fortress. King Saul's armor is stored here behind the temple and I do not understand why that must be, but we must allow it.

"So you can see there are many unanswered questions here and much fearful history. I do not wish to further disturb my priestesses or my life here."

CHAPTER 34

David's mouth dropped open. He hid his face in his hands for a few moments.

"Laila, I did not know these things. God knows I have been running for my life from Saul until he died on the battle field. If you will allow me, I will take his armor from this place and have it buried with his body, and it will be of no more concern to you."

Laila thought for a few minutes. If the armor were removed then perhaps Ishtara would come back even if for only short visits and be at peace. It would be so good to have her here and they could laugh and sing again. She turned to David who was waiting patiently.

"Yes, please take Saul's armor away and relieve us of the awful reminder."

"I will call two of my men and we will do it immediately and quietly."

He signaled to his two guards. Laila showed them where the armor was stored behind the temple. They pulled it out, wrapped it in a robe, bowed respectfully to David and Laila, and carried it out of the gate. David and Laila hesitated for a moment at the gate.

"Thank you, David. You have been a friend this evening and I will remember it."

"I will not come to your gate again unless invited. If you need me, I will come."

He stepped through the gate. She bowed to the king and he left.

Ishtara and Jarib's twins were born at the Temple of Astarte so the midwife could attend them. It was not an easy birth, but all was well with the infants and Ishtara. It seemed a very short time after they returned to Endor that Ishtara knew something in her body was again changing.

"It cannot be happening again already!"

Ishtara left the twins with Rébekah and the elderly priestesses from the village and returned to the temple. Abigail smiled and summoned the midwife.

"Yes, it often happens soon after a birth if the couple does not wait for a woman's body to close the womb and realign itself. It seems you were a bit eager! Most couples are after months of not coming together."

The midwife left with her apology for speaking out to a High Priestess. Laila and Abigail laughed and soon Ishtara was laughing with them. They spent a few more days together and then Ishtara felt it was time to return to Endor. Abigail went with her to see the twins again and be of whatever help she could.

Jarib was waiting for Ishtara in the doorway of Rébekah's hut and reached out to embrace her and greet Abigail.

"It is good that you have returned. Rébekah has fallen ill and the elderly priestesses from Endor have been caring for her. They took the twins to the Village of Endor so Rébekah could rest. She asks for you daily and I assured her that you would come soon."

Ishtara and Abigail went immediately to Rébekah's bedside. Indeed, Rébekah looked very pale and much older. She reached up and took their hands.

"I am happy to see you. I feared I would leave before you could return."

"I stayed at the Temple of Astarte to see the midwife and to help Laila, now the High Priestess, put things in order before I left. I do not plan to return there to reside. I will stay here with Jarib and we will make our lives here together as you and Adaiah did so long ago."

Rébekah closed her eyes and smiled.

"I see your daughter is coming as the cosmic mothers said. I will not be here to see her. I will soon be with my dear beloved Adaiah."

She raised herself shakily on one elbow.

"I have news! The High Priest of Ba'al was murdered in his sleep and it seems that the dark energy has now gathered in and stayed within Ba'al's temple as it should and the evil part of it is dissipating. The darkness once again takes its proper place in the mysteries and threatens no more.

"I am guessing that you must have broken his heart when you escaped, Ishtara, and he lost the power to fool the priests that he was Ba'al, himself. There are new priests there now at Ba'al's temple who honor its true purpose. They are repairing the walls and restoring the gardens, and balancing it with the light of Astarte."

Ishtara and Abigail laughed with delight. Their time with Rébekah promised to be one of celebration and gathering of the light. They would all fly together into the cosmic realms and taste the glories of the greater world.

It was a new and marvelous experience for Jarib, whose world had been as Samuel decreed it. He was ready for the expansion of his consciousness into the heavenly realms as well. He sat patiently with them in the Sacred Circle and focused his mind on Yahweh asking to see the greater way.

To Jarib's delight and satisfaction he could feel that cosmic lifting and his expanding inner vision that new no boundaries. He realized, too, that this capacity was within everyone. People could learn how to access it and how to expand their own spiritual experience. He allowed Ishtara and Abigail to teach him about the Secret Way. He was not quite able to reliably produce it himself, but he could now travel safely on the energies with Ishtara.

A few months later there was a gathering in the cosmic realm of those who had gone on. Majah, Adaiah, Samuel, and others came to the bedside of Rébekah to witness her passing and take her spirit into the next expression in living with them. Rébekah smiled and joyfully declared she could see them all!

"Adaiah, I am coming my love! I am coming!"

She closed her eyes, smiled, gave a sigh of contentment and was gone.

Ishtara, Jarib, Abigail and some of the elderly priestesses carried her body to the Sacred Circle at the edge of the cliff. They built a fire and placed a rack over it. They placed her body on the rack and covered it with her favorite robe. They sang a ceremony of passing, placed flowers on the robe and repeated a blessing together.

When the fire went out they removed the robe. Her body was gone, consumed completely. The robe immediately disintegrated in their hands and blew away as dust in the wind.

They picked up the flowers that had fallen to the ground. Sadly and joyfully at the same time, they walked together back through the woods to what had been Rébekah's hut. The priestesses created a meal and they all sat down together to savor all she had meant in their lives.

Ishtara and Jarib had much to do to renovate the old hut and create their own living quarters. Abigail could not bear to leave so they welcomed her to stay in Rébekah's part of the hut. She would happily care for the twins and help Ishtara through her last months before their daughter was born.

People came in from the Village of Endor to help with the construction. The men put up the walls for the center and the women created the living spaces for visitors and guests. Some cleared brush and rocks to smooth and enlarge the grounds to accommodate outdoor activities and gatherings and planted gardens of flowers and vegetables. Closer to the Village of Endor there were areas smoothed for pastures and shelters for sheep and goats.

Abigail joyfully presided over the retreat center that she named The Spirit of Rébekah, created activities, and planned to have spiritual retreats to the Sacred Circle for all levels of cosmic experience. She was getting on in years too, but felt rejuvenated at the thought of a new spiritual work.

Jarib gathered his priesthood brothers and the ones from Mount Carmel and together they built a small temple at Nob. It was the original place of the priests of Ahimelech, before King Saul had all the priests slaughtered and all the village people as well.

Saul thought Ahimelech was siding with David against him. Ahimelech actually knew nothing of the trouble between King Saul and David. King David would be happy that Jarib honored Ahimelech and the Village of Nob that was destroyed by King Saul's rage.

Jarib and his brothers from Mount Carmel were eager to begin training priests there in the name of Eli, Samuel, and God Creator of All. Their first students were Jarib and Ishtara's young twin sons Jair and Jamin. They were excited to start their training to be priests like their father. The word spread and attracted more young boys from surrounding communities who wanted to become priests too.

Brother Ammon and his brother priests from Mount Carmel Monastery supplied scrolls, writing tablets, bedding and food. King David sent servants to assist them and to keep them safe. Among them was Malachi, who was elderly and very lame, but greatly desired to be there until he passed on.

Jarib provided special quarters for him and reverently welcomed him.

"What can I do for you, my dear friend Malachi?"

"You can take me to see everything you have done here and I want to meet Majah's grandchildren. I have seen her granddaughter, Deborah, and now I want to see her grandsons, Jair and Jamin. I loved Majah and Ishtara. They are the only family I consider as if they were mine."

CHAPTER 35

Jarib took Malachi's arm and slowly walked with him around the school, in and out of the rooms, showing him the library and all that had been accomplished. Then they went out into the yard where Jair and Jamin were sitting on a bench under a tree in an intense conversation.

"These are my sons, Jair and Jamin. This is Malachi, your mother and grandmother's dear friend and protector."

They jumped up and bowed politely to Malachi.

"We are very happy to meet you. Mother has told us the stories of how you kept her safe from King Saul."

"It became my life's purpose to take care of them and you all are my rewards for being successful. I only wish I could have saved your grandmother, Majah."

Jair almost had tears in his eyes as he stepped forward and embraced Malachi.

"Dear Malachi, many sad things have happened, but we are here now and we will continue living in the highest possible way. King David is our champion and all will be well. You will live here with us and we will care for you in whatever way you need. You are our family, too."

Jamin stepped forward shyly. Malachi reached out to him and they embraced. Jarib was so pleased that his sons welcomed Malachi into their family. He felt the same way.

"No doubt Rébekah will be watching over you until you join the heavenly throng?"

Malachi laughed out loud.

"Indeed she will. I watched over her for many years. It is her turn now."

Jarib returned to Endor to share with Ishtara the wonderful progress the school was making, and how Jair and Jamin welcomed the arrival of Malachi.

"Malachi! He is there! I must return with you to see him! How wonderful that he will be with all of you!"

"King David saw to it that he was delivered to us by royal carriage and we created living quarters for him. Our sons took him in as family immediately."

Deborah, Ishtara and Jarib's daughter, overheard the conversation.

"I want to go too! I want to see Jair and Jamin, even though they chase me and pull my hair. When I am twelve and I can go to the Temple of Astarte, and they will have to respect me at a priestess. Please, Mother, will you and father take me to see them and see Malachi again?"

"Yes, we will take you with us. We have much to accomplish here and then we will go."

"How long will that take?"

"Deborah, you must have a little patience. Why not help us with the things we need to do?"

"Yes, I will help if it will make everything go faster."

Jarib shook his head and went to see Abigail. She was sitting with the three elderly priestesses from the Village of Endor. They came in a wagon pulled by two small donkeys. Though frail and unsteady, they wished to see and experience all that Abigail had accomplished. Ishtara saw her opportunity to expose Deborah to the life of priesthood and asked the elderly ones to speak with her. They were delighted!

"Deborah, would you please take the priestesses around and show them the grounds before you bring them into the dining room?"

Deborah looked in dismay at the old women who had climbed carefully out of the wagons with the help of the gardeners. She glanced helplessly at Ishtara and then back to the priestesses.

"You are Deborah, are you not? I am Annat and these are Marah and Josie. Your grandmother was very precious to us, as is your mother. Let us walk to the Sacred Circle and sit down to talk."

Deborah looked around for Jarib, but he and Abigail were somewhere else. She hoped they would not leave for Nob without her. Obediently she followed after the priestesses through the woods to the Sacred Circle. They sat down close together and Annat began.

"Deborah, have you thought about being one of us as a priestess of Astarte?"

"Yes, that is my mother's wish. She is a High Priestess you know."

"Yes, we do know that. But it must be your desire as well. Let us show you some of the powers of a priestess and how they can be used to bless and heal."

Annat created a Sacred Way for herself and Deborah and aimed it at the gate of the Temple of Astarte. She took Deborah's hand and both stood up. In an instant Deborah was standing before the temple gate with Annat. She looked around in amazement.

"How did we get here? What is this place?"

"We came by the energy wave I created called the Secret Way. That is how we travel sometimes. This is the great Temple of Astarte, where all the priestesses are trained in the celestial and cosmic arts. You will make many lifelong friends here with priestesses who will always be at your side. We are a divine sisterhood that is never broken. The world can be lonely and cruel, but not here. We practice the great love of Astarte here and share that love with each other and those who need us for healing and comfort."

Laila came to the gate when she saw Annat and Deborah.

"Annat, is all well at Endor?"

"Yes, Laila, all is well. I brought Deborah to show her our great temple and to tell her something of the life of a priestess. Of course I brought her by the Sacred Way. We will return to Endor shortly."

"Do you want to come in?"

"I am sure that will not be appropriate as yet. Deborah must make up her mind and I wanted to give her something to think about in regard to that choice. Her grandmother and mother were brought here as orphans, but it is different for Deborah. She has a family, which they did not, and is coming of the age to make her own choice."

"Does Ishtara know she is here?"

"Yes, she does. And she knows I will not violate our temple rules and boundaries. Deborah may enter if she decides to become a priestess and when she is ready."

"I agree. I am so pleased to see you both and I will pray for your progress, Deborah, whatever you decide that shall be."

Annat and Deborah stepped into the Secret Way and were instantly in the Sacred Circle. Marah and Josie told Deborah their life stories as priestesses and how it felt in their hearts to worship the love of Astarte.

Deborah was more than a little overwhelmed by it all. But she listened with great fascination. She had not even thought to worry about her parents going to Nob without her.

"Thank you all for telling me all these things and for taking me to the temple. It is all so helpful. I feel different already and I must think about all of this."

"Thank you is all you need to say. We can always visit again if there is more you want to ask. There is much for you to take in and we understand. We know you are anxious to go to Nob to see your brothers, now. Be at peace and let all you have seen and heard sink into your consciousness. When the time is right you will know what choice to make."

Jarib and Ishtara were ready to return to Nob when Deborah came back with the priestesses. Deborah was in a somewhat somber mood, no longer acting like a child demanding that her parents to hurry. Ishtara saw the change. The protective barrier of childhood consciousness gave away and Deborah was released to mature beyond it.

"Thank you dear sisters for helping Deborah understand a little better who we are and what her heritage is. Sometimes a mother needs a little help and I am sure you did a better job than I could under the circumstances. To her I am not a High Priestess, just her mother. I love you all."

They all sat down for a meal together before the three would leave for Nob. Deborah was famished after her experiences of the afternoon. She still had one more question.

"Father, who were Rébekah and Malachi?"

"We will be seeing Malachi in Nob and he will tell you all about Rébekah. Let us finish and we will go."

CHAPTER 36

Deborah ran into her brothers' arms and they danced and laughed. Malachi was on hand to greet her as well.

"Come to me after the evening meal, Deborah, and I will tell you all about your grandmother and your mother and the saga of our time surviving King Saul."

"You must tell me all about Rébekah too!"

"That I will surely do."

She toured the monastery with Jair and Jamin, fascinated by the library and the other boys who were studying there. She asked them many questions about their training and studies, and why they wanted to be priests. They were happy to share their stories and asked her if she would be a priest, too.

"No silly, priests are boys, men, and priestesses are women. I may become a priestess of the Temple of Astarte."

It seemed a little odd that they studied about Yahweh, and not Astarte, but they explained that to her.

"Ishtara will come to teach us about Astarte and about the realm of the gods and goddesses. She will tell them that all of these realms live within us and how they all come together in the One. We are always excited to hear her lessons!"

Jair and Jamin were surprised at Deborah, who not too long ago was their bratty little sister, and now she was suddenly different! She was growing up and they were actually enjoying her company.

Deborah was open and eager to hear what Malachi had to say and went to find Malachi after dinner. Jair directed her to his room.

"Welcome, Deborah! Come in and sit down. There is much I want to tell you and I am sure much you want to know. Here, sit here beside me. Let us begin with your grandmother, Majah."

Deborah leaned forward completely engrossed in all Malachi was telling her. It was nearly dark when Jair came for her.

"We need to go to our rooms for the night, Deborah. Perhaps Malachi can speak with you again tomorrow."

"I am happy to speak you, Deborah, tomorrow and anytime. Good night, my dear. Sleep well."

"Thank you, Malachi, I will. And thank you for all you told me."

Jarib and Ishtara met Deborah and Jair in a common room.

"Deborah, our rooms are here right next to each other. So call if you need something."

"I will mother or should I say 'My Lady, High Priestess of Astarte!'"

"Mother is good. You still must obey me. Now off to bed."

Jair departed and Jarib joined Ishtara in their room. They spoke in whispers.

"It seems our daughter is growing up quickly. What has happened to cause this sudden maturity?"

"When the priestess Annat took her to the Temple of Astarte by the Secret Way. The other elderly priestesses shared their stories with her as well. She was mightily impressed. They also told her the decision was hers to make at the right time."

"Did they show her around the temple?"

"No they could not. The rule is that only priestesses enter the temple and Deborah is not a priestess. So they remained outside of the gate and spoke with Laila briefly. They then returned to Endor."

Back at Endor, Deborah begged Ishtara to teach her more about the arts of the priestesses.

"Please, mother, I must know more before I can make a decision."

"You are basing your decision upon the wrong things, Deborah. The arts are not intended to entice you to become a priestess. They are not for your pleasure or to have powers that you can use for your entertainment. I know that would not be your intent, but the temptation is great and without the training of the priesthood at the Temple of Astarte, you would be in great danger. The darkness of Ba'al found me and without the training I would have been lost to that evil. I did the wrong thing against my training and was lost in the desert. With my early training I did manage to survive and return to the Temple of Astarte unharmed. It was a good lesson but a terrible experience."

"But the Temple of Ba'al is no longer evil. The priests there are good and do only good. Why would I be in danger?"

"Because evil did not begin with the Temple of Ba'al. Evil is in the hearts of mankind and can manifest at any time, especially in places of power. King Saul did much evil. Had he found me, he would have had me stoned to death. He had many women killed trying to find me. He had an evil spirit that raged within him, and he even tried to kill King David when David was just a young a boy."

"So I must decide first to be a priestess. Is that my only choice?"

"No, you can move into the Village of Endor, or Ramah with Samuel's kin, or near Nob, and live like an ordinary woman of a village. There are caravans that you could travel with to see other lands, but you would need a husband or protector."

"Were you happy as a priestess? Were you happy in temple life?"

"Yes, I was extremely happy. Laila and Abigail were my wonderful sisters and still are. They cared for me and trained me. We were together almost all the time and loved each other's company. But I was an orphan when I was taken there. It was the only thing my parents, Ana and Tolah, could do to keep me safe and see that I was raised in a place of love."

"May I go to the Sacred Circle and think on all you have said? Would that be a good thing to do?"

"That would be good. Remember to ask for understanding, not demand your own way. The Sacred Circle is about understanding only. I will ask Abigail to go with you and stay close by. It is a powerful place of cosmic energies and you should not be there alone."

Abigail and Deborah walked through the woods to the Sacred Circle.

"I will not be too close, but I will be where you can see me. You can ask me anything. I will keep a calm space around you and you can tell me when you are ready to return to Rébekah's place."

Deborah sat down on a bench in the Sacred Circle. Abigail placed herself a short distance away. She could feel Abigail clearing the atmosphere and it had a wonderful calming effect.

After a while Deborah dozed off and had a dream of Rébekah, Majah, Samuel and Adaiah all coming to her aid and lifting her up. They left a message in her mind as she awakened.

"We will always be with you. Tell no one of your dreams."

She sat for a short while taking in the dream. It all sounded so familiar even the message to tell no one. Presently she waved to Abigail and they started back through the woods.

At dinner Deborah was silent. She just had no words and no one asked her about her time in the Sacred Circle. Ishtara was certain she knew what had happened, but kept it to herself. A dream…tell no one about the dreams.

CHAPTER 37

Deborah made her decision. She wanted the love and community of priestesses. She wanted to know about heavenly things. She wanted to be in that cosmic realm and bring good to the earth.

"You are sure?"

"Yes, mother, I have never been more certain of anything except perhaps the love you and Jarib have for me."

"Then tomorrow we will go to the temple and I will present you."

"Will you stay there with me for a little while, or will you visit me?"

"I will leave you with Laila and she will introduce you to your new friend and the priestesses in training. You will be very busy and will not need me to be there. The experience is for you and you alone. You need not lean on me or Jarib. Are you ready to stand on your own as a priestess and create that same bond we have with other priestesses?"

"I have not thought of it quite in that way, but yes I am sure. It will be a very new experience for me, but I know you and father are always there even though far away. You will be in my heart every step of my way, as Malachi, Samuel, and grandmother have been with you. You have given me everything I need and I am ready."

Jarib came to join them as Ishtara prepared to escort Deborah to the temple by the Secret Way.

"We are so proud of you, Deborah! Know that your mother and I will always be here for you when you need us and we will see you again when it is the appropriate time. We love you and always will."

"I love you both more than I can say. I hope Jair and Jamin will be proud of me, too. I will earn their respect and trust and we will share a wonderful future, all of us together."

Ishtara took their daughter to the Temple of Astarte, to be trained as a priestess. They traveled on foot as Ishtara had and arrived at the gate to be admitted. Laila, now the High Priestess, was delighted to see Ishtara again and to welcome Deborah to the temple and the life of a priestess.

Laila asked Deborah the same questions that Abigail had asked young Hodesha, and Deborah responded with a heart-felt yes to all of them. She took Deborah into the temple and introduced her to her friend and trainer, Miriam. They greeted each other joyfully, and Miriam led Deborah away to show her around the temple and share the purification bath with her.

"Your name is now Judiah. Judiah forever. No longer Deborah."

Deborah was surprised, and then she remembered something about her mother's name being changed, but she did not know what Ishtara's first name was. It was never spoken.

"Judiah, you must never ask about your mother's first name. She is Ishtara and you are Judiah forever. Please remember that from how on you will not respond to the name Deborah in any way. We will train you. Do not worry."

Laila and Ishtara walked into the gardens and sat down together near the altar in the garden of flowers with some wine and bread to joyfully share all the wonder and joy they had always felt for each other and for the temple.

"It seems so long since we have been together, Ishtara. I have missed you every day. I have news for you. King David came here and removed King Saul's armor. His men took it to Saul's grave and buried it there. You can come here in peace."

"King David came here? What brought him here?"

"You know what brought him here, Ishtara. He has never forgotten me from the time we spoke at the monastery on Mount Carmel. I reminded him that we could not come together, ever. He said he knew that, but he wanted to assure me that he would protect the temple and would come to assist me if I needed help. I looked into his mind and saw no guile there.

"Then I told him the history of the attacks on us from the Temple of Ba'al and he was appalled. Of course he knew nothing of that and of King Saul's assault upon us. I told him that Saul's armor was brought here and it was still a source of pain. He and his men took it away."

"Did you tell him that I am Saul's daughter?"

"No. There is no need for him or anyone else to know that. Nor will I ever mention it to you again. Now, tell me all about the monastery at Nob and Abigail's work at Rébekah's at Endor."

"You must come and see it all for yourself. Come to Endor and we will go to Nob where Jarib works with the brothers of Mount Carmel while they train our sons to be priests. They will love to see you!

"Abigail is well and content. The elderly priestesses at the Village of Endor assist her when they are able and would very much like to see you again. What will Deborah's new name be?"

"It will be Judiah. I hope you approve."

"I do approve, not that my approval is necessary. I am sure she will carry it well and change all the sorrow of the past to joy."

Laila and Ishtara talked on into the evening, dined with the priestesses and Deborah, laughed and sang as they always did.

Ishtara kissed Deborah a tearful goodbye. Laila and Ishtara hugged and kissed each other's cheeks. Reluctantly they parted as Ishtara stepped into the Secret Way and returned to Endor.

Jarib was waiting for Ishtara.

"Did all go well with Deborah? Do you think she is happy with her decision?"

"She is wonderfully happy! Just as Laila has been my dear friend and trainer, so Deborah has one as well named Miriam. Deborah's name is now Judiah. So we will never speak the name Deborah again."

Jarib smiled at that. He had not quite understood why the name change, except it was meant to symbolize leaving the past life behind and a new consciousness to carry forward.

"I will try to remember and not say the name Deborah. We must be sure to tell Jair and Jamin and all who know her at Nob that Deborah is now Judiah forever, and never to speak the name Deborah. I am sure all the cosmic mothers will be pleased that she is becoming a priestess and will visit her often when she is ready to receive that which comes from the cosmic realms."

Jarib never asked Ishtara what her parents had first named her. He was beginning to learn about the energies and higher consciousness. Ishtara was not only the woman he loved, his wife and mother of his children, she was much more. She was an Ishtarati, High Priestess of all gods and goddesses.

No one knew of grandmother Majah's origins, but Majah had given her daughter the name Ishtara because she knew something of these Highest Heavens. She knew Ishtara was of the realm of Ishara, Ashtart, Inanna, and Ishtar. Her precinct was of the Highest Heavens and the Morning and Evening Star come down to earth. She was the female figure in a male dominated religious environment, even though El Shaddai was feminine aspect of Yahweh.

Jarib spent many long nights awake under the stars trying to fathom the whole complexity of these things. As he fell asleep one night Samuel appeared in his dreams.

"Jarib, do not be afraid to open yourself to the realms of God, the One over All. Walk with Ishtara through those realms and receive with her the blessings of being one with God."

Jarib awakened just as dawn was coming and looked around for Samuel. Then he knew it was a dream.

"Jarib, what has happened? You look startled. Are you all right?"

"Yes, I am all right. Just a dream. It was Samuel telling me not to be afraid to walk through the celestial realms with you and be at one with God. Is there more you need to tell me?"

"The celestial realms are not where we live, Jarib. They are the higher understanding that we draw from for our lives right here. Have you been afraid?"

"Not exactly afraid, just unsure of what comes next. Am I to walk alone or are we on this journey together? I have a hard time keeping the balance in my mind between the monastery and the temple. I know they are not at odds, but I do not always know how to put it together."

"We have put it together in our children, Jair and Jamin in the monastery and Judiah in the temple. They likely will have no trouble seeing it all as one. We began much of our challenges with these things in our adulthood and have had to struggle to understand through wars and attacks, but they are starting in their much younger years, in a time of peace, and from the same family.

"You and I are still priest and priestess, husband and wife, teachers and healers. We still live our lives on earth, but as spiritually aware of higher things. Our children are our arrows that shoot far ahead of us and where they are going we cannot follow, but we can pray for and support them in any way we can, especially with our love."

Jarib and Ishtara got up and walked hand in hand out into the cool dawn. Everything seemed freshly alive around them as if it were truly a new day.

CHAPTER 38

King David desired to see Laila once more. He sent her a message begging her to meet him at the Village of Endor rather than at the temple. He needed to know some things about the village and its history. She had begun to trust him and allow their friendship to continue to a certain point, but never would she reveal all that she was as a High Priestess of cosmic energies.

Reluctantly she created the Secret Way to Rébekah's. She would walk back to the village and meet him a little farther down the mountain path, so he would not actually enter it. The villagers would be much disturbed if the king arrived there.

He arrived an hour later and she met him in a clearing along the road. He alighted from the carriage and they sat on a step on the side of it.

"I do not know what you want to know or what I can tell you. What is so important that we should meet this way?"

"Laila, there are others who will come after me as kings and they will follow the edicts of Deuteronomy concerning sorcery. They will seek to destroy your temple and I will not be here to stop them or protect the temple. You and I will be long gone the way of the fathers and mothers. But while I am king you are safe.

"I have many wives and children, but you are the goddess of my life, if Yahweh will forgive me for saying so. You are the one I cannot live with, or live without. I think of you every day and night."

Laila moved a little further away from him and looked into his mind. There were dark clouds of worry but nothing more at least for the moment.

"David, what is on your mind? What disturbs you other than just the impossibility of our hearts desires?"

"Endor disturbs me or rather what I do not know about it. Will you tell me about Endor? Is there sorcery there? What is its connection to the Temple of Astarte?"

Laila was taken aback. She did not expect to be questioned about sorcery in connection with Endor, but then why else would he insist upon meeting near the Village of Endor. What should she tell him? Surely not about the Sacred Circle and the Secret Way or the Higher Heavens! He did not even know how she traveled to Endor today.

"Please, Laila, tell me so I can answer fools who question me about it, only looking to trap me and condemn it and you."

Laila sat quietly for several minutes trying to compose her thoughts.

"David, there are many in the world who seek power over others by pretending to do magic and sorcery. They take money from the people who long to see their dead loved ones again and leave them disappointed. They ward off any threat of attack upon themselves by claiming to have some kind of dark power that will cast an evil spell if people try to expose them. King Saul had this kind of fear that someone was casting spells upon him, as you may know from his violent outbursts. None of this was or is happening at Endor or the Temple of Astarte."

"There are priestesses here, are there not?"

"Yes, there are sweet elderly priestesses who have retired from the temple and are here to do only good for the people of Endor. They come here to spend their last days caring for the people. They do not cast evil spells. The teachings of Astarte are about love and healing, injuring no one."

Laila was sure she could not tell him about Ishtara's friendship with Samuel, or the great cosmic realms in which they all travel. She must avoid that at all costs.

"Is this all you can tell me, Laila? I want to know everything."

"David, Yahweh has lead you throughout your life, kept you safe, made you victorious in battle and crowned you king. I cannot hope to understand the ways of your god because I did not grow up in your world.

"I cannot teach you all the ways of Astarte, goddesses and priestesses because you did not grow up in my world. I can only tell you they all come together in the One God of All in ways too high for us to know. But we must trust that it is all good and not fight wars or injure people because we do not understand everything.

"The writers of the laws of Deuteronomy must have had a specific threat in mind, much of which came out of Egypt and other foreign powers that meant them harm. I am sure they were not meant to harm innocent people."

"I am thrilled that Jarib has built a monastery at Nob to honor Eli, Samuel, and all the priests that were slain there. Will you tell me about his wife, Ishtara? Is she a priestess?"

Again Laila swallowed hard. She wondered what he could be looking for. She scanned his mind and still found no guile, only worry. But what could his interest in Ishtara be?

"Ishtara is my dearest friend and the former High Priestess of the Temple of Astarte. She conferred the office of High Priestess upon me when she decided to retire from the temple and work with Jarib. They go often to Nob where their sons are training to become priests of Yahweh."

She desperately did not want to tell him that Ishtara and Jarib lived at Rébekah's retreat or to take him there, which he would surely want to do.

"David, it is getting late and I must return to the temple now. Perhaps we can talk another time."

"Yes. I will take you to the temple in my carriage if you will allow me."

She agreed in order to avoid having to make up a story about how she would travel there. By carriage would take much longer than the Secret Way. The idea of sitting beside him in the carriage for a few hours or more gave her feelings about him that she would rather keep at bay. She knew how challenging it would be to keep her mind on higher things and not give in to the urges of her body.

The carriage had side curtains which David drew shut when the evening brought a chill, and twilight and darkness would soon come. His driver slowed the carriage to avoid the ruts and rocks that were becoming hard to see.

In the darkness inside the carriage, David put his hand on her thigh and she trembled. He drew her close and kissed her neck and her shoulder. She wanted to draw away, but his lips found hers and she could only melt into his arms.

"Tell me now if you want me to stop, Laila, and I will leave the carriage and ride my horse the rest of the way."

She could only return his caresses and whisper that he should stay. He gently pushed her tunic aside and moved down to kiss her body. She moaned as he entered her and all the passion of their waiting and dreaming exploded into ecstasy over and over.

At the temple gate they reluctantly released each other. He helped Laila from the carriage and opened the gate for her. Resolutely she walked in step by step not daring to look back at him. She breathed a sigh of relief when she heard the gate shut and his carriage roll away, followed by his horses and guards.

She went immediately to her bath and called for the midwife to bring herbs to prevent a pregnancy. She kept whispering to herself over and over.

"This must not happen ever again."

But the words felt like ashes in her mouth. She prayed to Astarte to be merciful, that he would stay away, and not summon her again. Ashes of despair.

The next week she went to Endor to tell Ishtara that David was asking about her and about sorcery. They sat in the Sacred Circle together discussing all that was said.

"Do not worry, Laila. Rébekah and I caused Saul to think he was talking to Samuel, when he was actually talking to Jarib. We committed deception, but no sorcery. We did not claim it was Samuel. It was Saul who decided it was Samuel and called out to him. But now Saul is gone and the story is like the wind. It had no substance or truth.

"Now Laila, I cannot look into your mind. I never chose to learn to do that, but still I know that more happened between you and David than just talking about me."

"Since the rescue from the Amalekites and the meeting on Mount Carmel, you know I have been drawn to him. And then he came to the temple and removed Saul's armor. I have fought that feeling all this time. He offered to take me back to the temple in his carriage and I could not tell him I would return by the Secret Way! I guess I knew then that my resistance was futile and I was in his arms. Our passion knew no bounds. It had been held at bay too long."

"Did you call for the midwife and some herbs?"

"Yes! I am too old to have a child and what would I do with one? And King David's child of all people!"

"No one needs to know that, Laila. I know you feel exposed and vulnerable now, but there is nothing to fear. If it has happened inside of you, you would not be the first priestess to have a child. How would we keep the temple populated if we did not? Astarte is the goddess of fertility!"

They both broke up laughing and returned from the circle to Rébekah's hut and dinner. Jarib looked at Ishtara and then at Laila, and knew something was up, but this time he knew not to ask. All would eventually be revealed. He smiled to himself and poured another cup of wine for them all.

CHAPTER 39

Abigail suddenly passed away. She had spoken of her illness to only a few. She would go to the priestesses in the Village of Endor for their ministrations, but she knew her time was coming. The villagers from Endor, priestesses from the Temple of Astarte, priests from Nob, Ishtara and Jarib all participated in her ceremony as she passed on. Her ashes were lovingly scattered in the Sacred Circle where she always desired to be and now to rest.

Jarib and Ishtara traveled to Nob. Jarib was becoming accustomed to the Secret Way. He would tease Ishtara to make it high enough so his feet did not drag on the ground.

They took the sad news of Abigail's passing to Malachi and he wept.

"We are all going, Ishtara, and soon you will be the last sorceress at Endor! Oh, I mean priestess! I am teasing."

"Yes, I am sure to be the last, Malachi. Endor will no longer be in danger from kings or sought out by magicians looking for a place to practice their evil. It will be seen as the clean beautiful village it has always been. It will be a retirement place for elderly priestesses where they can live in community with each other."

The elderly priestesses in the Village of Endor promised to watch over The Spirit of Rébekah retreat that Abigail had established. Ishtara stayed at Nob to be with her sons and teach spirituality to the student priests for Jarib. The students were eager for her classes and thrilled to hear about the Temple of Astarte, the Higher Heavens, the Sacred Way, and the Sacred Circle. They wanted to know how to access their higher minds and the spiritual pathway to Yahweh. As Ishtara had told Jarib, it was all coming together in their children and their students.

Malachi would hobble into her classes, and when he could not, the students carried him on a litter. It brought tears to Ishtara's eyes to see how much they loved and cared for him. He stood between her and death so many times, and now she was standing with him as he faced his.

He told them the stories about grandmother Majah, about Saul's hunt for Majah's child, and Saul's demand to see a medium, a woman with a spirit, a sorceress. The students were riveted to their seats, leaning in toward him and his stories. Still, no one ever revealed that Ishtara was the daughter that King Saul was frantically looking for, and amazingly no one thought to ask.

"When I die, please take me to Ramah to be with Samuel, Jarib. That is the only place where I will rest and be at peace."

"I promise you we will do that. Let me help you back to your room."

Actually, Jarib carried the thin emaciated Malachi to his room. He placed him gently on his bed and covered him with a robe. He sat with him for a while silently thanking him for Ishtara and all he had done for them. As he got up to leave, Malachi spoke his name.

"Jarib. Thank you."

Malachi gave a sigh and breathed no more. He was gone.

Jarib stopped and turned to blow out the candle in the corner of the room. He decided to wait until morning to tell Ishtara and make arrangements to take him to Ramah.

All of Nob mourned his passing, especially Ishtara. She built the fire and placed a grid over it. Malachi's body was tenderly placed on it and he was covered with his robe. They caught his ashes in an urn and took them to Ramah. With tears in their eyes, they placed the sealed urn in a niche beside the tomb of Samuel, and returned to Nob.

The next several months at the monastery were quiet without Malachi, and then a visitor arrived by the Secret Way. It was Laila carrying a precious bundle, her child.

Ishtara ran to embrace her and reached for the baby. They sang and cooed over him as they talked of what to do next. It was a boy child and could not be raised at the Temple of Astarte.

Jarib came to greet Laila and took the baby from Ishtara for the pleasure of holding an infant again.

"His name is Eli after Samuel's mentor."

"If you will allow me, Laila, I know the most wonderful couple who lost their child not too long ago, and they could take him until he is old enough to live at the monastery."

Jair and Jamin arrived on the scene to see the baby.

"Laila, we will be his brothers, and we will care for him. Eli! You are now our brother forever."

"You are young boys. How would you know how to care for a baby?"

"Well, someone could show us how, like you, Mother and Father!"

Jarib and Ishtara look at each other and burst out laughing.

"You three were enough!"

"Let me talk to this husband and wife. The wife could nurture a baby and as he grows, you brothers can take him on. You can visit him and he will know and love you as his brothers."

Naomi and Moshe were amazed and delighted to take Laila's child for a few years until he could be with the brothers at the monastery. Even when they brought him to the monastery it would not be like losing him as they had their child, because he would still be near them.

Jarib and Ishtara were patriarch and matriarch of a whole new family. Laila was thrilled to have a wonderful place for Eli. She would see him when she visited Ishtara and Jarib. Naomi and Moshe were happy to be part of this extended family and loved Laila immediately. Jair and Jamin stood by like sentries, ready to greet and defend their new little brother.

Laila and Ishtara went for a walk together to discuss Judiah's progress at the Temple of Astarte.

"She seems to have grandmother Majah's sense of the cosmic and learns quickly. She helps the other ones in training and creates ways to make them welcome and feel the enthusiasm that she has for all the studies.

"She was a great help to me during my morning sickness, taking on my duties that she did so easily. She held Eli whenever she could and was so sad to see me take him here to Nod. I may bring her with me for short visits, but careful not to interrupt her training."

"Have you seen David again? Does he know about Eli?"

"Yes, he knows. He sends a sealed message with a highly trusted envoy to inquire about both of us. He also knows that Malachi passed on. I will not see him again because I do not need to birth another child at my age. This one nearly killed me, but I lived through it thanks to our faithful midwife who knew what to do!"

"He will not take Eli into his service, will he?"

"No, he is content to leave Eli in the care of the monastery to become a priest. It is his way of giving back to Nob in recompense for all the destruction that Saul did here."

"Does he want Eli to know who his father is?"

"Really, he does not. David does not want him drawn into the politics of his world or compete for power with his other sons. They would surely harm and even kill him. He wants some part of himself to remain the innocent shepherd boy that he remembers with such fondness and longing."

"May it ever remain so, but Laila, just as my children are more and more making their own decisions, so will Eli come to that place in his life. If he ever finds out who his father is, he could hate us for not telling him and decide to claim his birthright."

"I know that, but I am depending upon the love we have here within our family to be powerful enough to keep him with us. I pray that David's other sons do not learn of Eli. They would surely come after him to destroy him. I just hope he does not grow up to look and act exactly like David and give himself away!"

"Yes, I barely survived looking and being like my mother, Majah."

"What will you do now, Ishtara? Where will you go? Will you stay here or go back to Endor, or come back to the Temple of Astarte?"

"I will make my home at Endor, Laila. I cannot come back to the temple except for a visit or special occasion. Young Judiah will make her own way and I do not want to interfere. I cannot stay here at the monastery, although Jarib would like that. Monasteries are for the men. I can teach the young priests about the mysteries and be here when he needs me.

"No, Endor has been my second home, my sacred place after the Temple. I will care for the elderly priestesses that come to the Village of Endor, keep the place sacred, and most likely be the last priestess of Endor."

They sat quietly together for a long time holding hands. They were Laila and Ishtara, friends in love forever. They embraced each other and kissed each other's cheeks, and Laila stepped into her Secret Way to return to the Temple of Astarte. Ishtara went to hold and kiss Jarib and her sons before she stepped into her Secret Way to return to Endor.

She gathered the elderly priestesses and they walked quietly together to the Sacred Circle to commune with the higher energies, the loved ones who were now in the Highest Heavens, and open themselves to the higher love and wisdom that always awaited them.

Ishtara basked in the love she had for this place and all that had brought her here. It was now hers to cherish and protect.

"Kings come and go, are crowned and killed, but Endor goes on eternally in the hearts of those who knew its true calling and lived it. All love to Astarte and Yahweh. Amen."

Printed in the United States
By Bookmasters